# A DOG'S
# PERFECT CHRISTMAS

W. Bruce Cameron is the number one *New York Times* and *USA Today* bestselling author of *A Dog's Purpose*, *A Dog's Journey* and *A Dog's Way Home* (all now major motion pictures), *A Dog's Promise*, *The Dog Master*, *Ellie's Story*, *Bailey's Story*, *Lily's Story*, *The Midnight Plan of the Repo Man*, and others. He lives in California.

D1341198

ACC. No: 05173230

# By W. Bruce Cameron

*A Dog's Purpose*
*A Dog's Journey*
*A Dog's Promise*
*Emory's Gift*
*The Dogs of Christmas*
*The Dog Master*
*A Dog's Way Home*
*A Dog's Perfect Christmas*

## THE RUDDY MCCANN SERIES

*The Midnight Plan of the Repo Man*
*Repo Madness*

## HUMOUR

*A Dad's Purpose*
*8 Simple Rules for Dating My Teenage Daughter*
*How to Remodel a Man*
*8 Simple Rules for Marrying My Daughter*

## FOR YOUNGER READERS

*Bailey's Story*
*Bella's Story*
*Ellie's Story*
*Lily's Story*
*Max's Story*
*Molly's Story*
*Shelby's Story*
*Toby's Story*

*Lily to the Rescue*
*Lily to the Rescue: Two Little Piggies*
*Lily to the Rescue: The Not-So-Stinky Skunk*
*Lily to the Rescue: Dog Dog Goose*

# A DOG'S PERFECT CHRISTMAS

## W. Bruce Cameron

PAN BOOKS

First published 2020 by Forge Books, Tom Doherty Associates, New York

First published in the UK 2020 by Pan Books
an imprint of Pan Macmillan
The Smithson, 6 Briset Street, London EC1M 5NR
Associated companies throughout the world
www.panmacmillan.com

ISBN 978-1-5290-1011-4

Copyright © W. Bruce Cameron 2020

The right of W. Bruce Cameron to be identified as the
author of this work has been asserted by him in accordance
with the Copyright, Designs and Patents Act 1988.

All rights reserved. No part of this publication may be reproduced,
stored in a retrieval system, or transmitted, in any form, or by any means
(electronic, mechanical, photocopying, recording or otherwise)
without the prior written permission of the publisher.

Pan Macmillan does not have any control over, or any responsibility for,
any author or third-party websites referred to in or on this book.

1 3 5 7 9 8 6 4 2

A CIP catalogue record for this book is available from the British Library.

Printed and bound by CPI Group (UK) Ltd, Croydon, CR0 4YY

MIX
Paper from
responsible sources
FSC
www.fsc.org
FSC® C116313

This book is sold subject to the condition that it shall not, by way of
trade or otherwise, be lent, hired out, or otherwise circulated without
the publisher's prior consent in any form of binding or cover other than
that in which it is published and without a similar condition including
this condition being imposed on the subsequent purchaser.

Visit **www.panmacmillan.com** to read more about all our books
and to buy them. You will also find features, author interviews and
news of any author events, and you can sign up for e-newsletters
so that you're always first to hear about our new releases.

For Eloise, Garrett, and Ewan

# A DOG'S PERFECT CHRISTMAS

# CHAPTER ONE

S ander opened his eyes and felt around internally for
his usual pains. Yes, they were there—the ache in his
sixty-seven-year-old knees, gifted to him by his high-
school job laying carpet. His arthritic fingers. The twist in
his lower back that was aggravated by lifting objects, or
sneezing, or moving, or not moving.

No one had ever told him that growing old would *hurt*
so much.

He turned his head and allowed himself to believe that
the mound of pillows on the other side of the mattress was
the silhouette of his wife, slumbering peacefully. Alive. But
he stared too long and another familiar pain, worse than all
the others, joined him in the night. Barbara had been dead
for more than two years.

He made his way to the bathroom, where it sometimes
seemed he spent more of his time than he did sleeping.
When he shuffled back to bed, something new bit at him
from within, and he sat on the edge of the mattress, massaging the area just over his heart and frowning. "Never felt
this one before," he muttered.

His dog, Winstead, stirred on the floor, reacting to Sander's voice by raising his head and staring into the gloom.

"Sort of a sharp, stabbing feeling," Sander advised the dog.

Maybe Winstead heard something in Sander's tones that alarmed him. At nine years old, he was senior for a wolfhound, so it was unusual that he roused himself and padded over to put his head on Sander's thigh. Sander reached down and scratched his dog's ear with a gentle finger, and Winstead leaned toward it with appreciation.

"Good boy," Sander whispered. He drew in a breath and let it out in a long, contemplative sigh. "God, I miss her." He glanced over at the row of pillows.

For a long time there was no sound but a quiet hum from the clock radio next to the bed.

"I wouldn't do it any different," Sander finally told his dog. "She got to stay at home, and she died in our bed, just the way she wanted. I never told her how much it was costing, the in-home care, or that I would have to sell the place once she was gone. She never would have allowed that." He shifted his attentions to the dog's other ear, and Winstead tilted that way. "I couldn't let her die in a hospital room."

After a long moment, Sander struggled out of the bed and sat in his big recliner, one of the few items of furniture that had made it when he moved in with his son's family. He put his hand on his chest, taking deep, diagnostic breaths. Winstead went back to his dog bed and collapsed into it with a groan.

"Okay," Sander said aloud. "This could be it."

Winstead thumped his tail once, not understanding.

The next morning Ello opened her grandfather's door with her heart pounding. He hadn't responded to her light tapping, and she was terrified he had Died In The Night and she would be the one to see it first.

Of all the emotions that had been rampaging through her system like drunk rioters since she'd turned thirteen—the fear, the anxiety, the angst, the rage—this was the worst. This . . . *dread*. The worst, and the most common. She felt it about everything—school, her clothes, friends—everything.

One of her teachers had told her that it was normal, when your hormones decided to attack the host organism, to be riding "a roller coaster of emotions." As if it were a joyride . . . as if you could stop every so often for a hot dog and cotton candy. But that wasn't how it felt to Ello. If she were indeed trapped in some sort of demonic amusement park from the land of insanity, it wasn't a roller coaster—it was a merry-go-round. Around and around she went, always the same ride, always a different horse.

Ello was carrying a tray with a cup of coffee, some perfectly fried eggs, toast, and a chicken sausage. This was what her Grandpa Sander consumed every morning of his life, brought to him by Ello as if she were a Servant In Her Own

House. Only the breakfast meat changed, on the whim of the kitchen. The sausage looked disgusting.

She always felt phobic when she knocked and opened her grandfather's door. This particular morning, Grandpa Sander sat slumped in his chair, with sallow skin and thin hair that had not seen the discipline of a comb for some time. To Ello, Sander's birch-bark skin matched his hair, which matched his lips, which matched his teeth.

She knew she was supposed to love him because he was her grandfather, but most of the time, she could not.

And now the dread was all-consuming because he wasn't moving. His eyes weren't completely shut either—*Gross!*—as if he'd passed away before he could fully close his lids. Ello stood perfectly still, wondering if this was the morning she'd always known would come. She glanced over at Winstead. Winstead also wasn't moving, also didn't appear to be breathing.

Maybe they were both dead. Maybe *Ello* was dead.

Would that be so bad? If she were dead, she wouldn't have to go to school and face the impossible, grinding pressure of eighth grade. She wouldn't have to endure the humiliation anymore. She could ascend to heaven with this platter of eggs as her offering and be escorted back to sixth grade, the last time she was truly happy, when all of her friends adored her and her boyfriend had bought her a Valentine's Day card with a chocolate heart before she broke up with him.

She heard the thunder of her brothers hitting the hallway like Santa Claus falling off the roof. In mere moments, the twins would either blow by the open doorway or veer in to inflict their havoc on Grandpa. They always did this, always woke up simultaneously, as if shocked awake by the same bolt of lightning.

Their choice today was Sander's bedroom. Garrett and Ewan, three-year-old identical twins, somehow made running into the room sound like a collision.

Grandpa reacted as if he'd been hit with a taser, all four of his limbs spasming as Garrett leapt into his lap. Winstead jerked in sympathetic detonation.

Ello decided that the old man was not dead.

"Which one are you?" Grandpa Sander inquired in a voice that did not sound as if he really cared about the answer.

"That's Garrett," Ello reminded him, setting the meal on the serving table next to the recliner.

"Cudory cad dah wee wowo!" Garrett shouted.

Sander frowned in disapproving noncomprehension.

"He says good morning, Grandpa, and he wants you to read him a story," Ello advised.

Ewan picked up a dog toy—a red rubber ball—and, yelling "Wenked!" threw it seemingly at random with all the propulsion his little arm could manage. It knocked down a framed photograph, like in one of those carnival games where you throw a ball at a stuffed clown, then bounced and landed with a muffled thud in the center of Grandpa's bed. Winstead flicked a single ear to signal that, under other circumstances, he might have been interested in this violent treatment of what was, after all, his toy.

Not for the first time, Ello wondered why the ball was red. She had learned at school that canines cannot see the color red at all. It seemed a cruel joke to play on a dog, much as her parents were playing a cruel joke on her, making her live here and do chores and go to school when She Had Never Asked To Be Born.

"Well, go away, Garrett," Grandpa instructed.

Ello smirked. As if it were that easy. As if the twins hadn't come breaking into their lives like axe murderers entering a farmhouse. "Okay, boys, go get your breakfast," she suggested.

The boys did leave, not so much because they were told to—they never did anything they were told to—but because the word "breakfast" reminded them that there was food to be flung at each other. They left at a sprint, but Ello lingered for a moment. As her father had mandated, she asked her grandfather if he needed anything.

Grandpa sourly regarded the plate next to his chair. "I don't seem to have much of an appetite this morning," he confessed. This was pretty much what he said every morning, so Ello did not respond.

God, she hated living here!

"Okay, goodbye," she said after a dismal moment.

The merry-go-round. Same place, same people, same conversation. The carousel horse of dread had bucked her off once Grandpa opened his eyes. Now Ello was riding the dour horse of apathy. Next would come breakfast, then school, then home, then repeat. It Was Pointless.

❄

The scent of sausage was so joyously thick on the air that Winstead was lifted out of bed and dragged across the room by it. He sat with all the good dog he could muster, focused on his person, who for some reason didn't respond by tossing chunks of food. Winstead could catch treats thrown in his direction—it was his special skill.

He thought of his person as "Daddy." That's what he had been taught from the time he was a puppy. "Go to Daddy! Come to Mommy! Give Daddy a kiss!"

By staring relentlessly, Winstead forced Daddy to lift his eyes. Excitement coursed through the dog; surely now they'd share this tantalizing meal.

Daddy raised his fork.

*Yes!*

He cut into the meat, releasing billows of delicious odors that rose from his plate like a flock of birds.

*Yes!*

He smiled at Winstead. "What, you want some of this?"

Time to roll out another trick. Winstead lowered his body to the floor, lying down in such a worthy fashion that he knew a piece of sausage would be the next item of business.

*Yes!*

Winstead snagged the chunk of meat and gulped it down so quickly he didn't have much of a chance to taste it. Now he stared again, waiting for an encore.

"Sometimes I think you're the only one left who loves me, Winstead," Daddy whispered.

Something in the voice, in the unknown words, broke Winstead's maniacal focus on the sausage. He'd heard that tone so often, lately. . . . When he pressed his body against Daddy's leg, he felt the mood radiating down the hand that momentarily stroked his head. *Sadness.* Daddy was sad, and Winstead couldn't seem to change that, no matter how good a dog he tried to be.

Juliana watched without comment as Ewan regarded his plastic fork with a devilish expression on his face. She knew exactly what was happening: her son was drawing a connection between the soft tines of his breakfast cutlery and some portion of his brother's anatomy. In a moment, Ewan would turn to his twin and stab something. The damage would mostly be to Juliana's eardrums as Garrett howled in protest, then escalated the conflict with a plateful of food heaved at Ewan's face.

"Ewan," Juliana warned, "don't you dare do anything with that fork besides use it to put scrambled eggs in your mouth."

Ewan's expression was one of frank assessment. *How had she known?*

Garrett was trying to squish his breakfast into a stegosaurus. "Garrett, stop playing with your food and eat it," Juliana instructed.

Garrett affected deafness and kept molding his eggs with Jurassic intent, his brother gazing on malevolently.

"What would happen," Juliana asked herself, idly and aloud, "if I just let them go ahead and kill each other?"

Would she be implicated in the crime? How could she have known—what reasonable mother would ever suspect that her sons harbored such homicidal designs toward each other?

*You could plead insanity,* her lawyer brain advised. People who talked to themselves were insane, right? Since they'd begun having children, Juliana had been chatting out loud to no one but her own self. Probably because she yearned so desperately to speak to an adult.

She sighed. A few days ago, she had wandered into the kitchen and found Ewan helping Garrett climb up on the counter to retrieve a chef's knife from its wooden block. They'd both giggled insanely when she admonished them. It was interesting that Ewan would participate so willingly in his own evisceration. Or maybe it wasn't that. Maybe they were planning to kill their parents, take the family car, and drive south from Traverse City to Miami Beach for spring break.

"Good morning, Ello," Juliana greeted her daughter as she shuffled into the kitchen. Like all girls her age, Ello had mastered the art of walking without picking her feet up off the floor. Conserving energy, Juliana supposed, for the next teenage tantrum.

Ello sat at the table without saying anything and dug methodically into her eggs. She pushed the sausage away with a look of utter scorn. She was going through a vegetarian phase, except for eggs, except for dairy products, except for steak.

"So, Ello," Juliana began.

Ello looked up with cold eyes and gave Juliana a sour, head-to-toe assessment. Ello was examining her mother's body, lingering on the post-pregnancy "orchestra and balcony," as Juliana's mother liked to say, and apparently finding fault with all she surveyed. To be fair, Juliana had given herself the same look that very morning—a critical examination in the mirror of what had happened to her once-taut physique since the twins had blown up her body from the inside and then so overtaken her daily schedule that she hadn't been to a gym in three years. Juliana used to hit the beach in a bikini. Then a one-piece. Next time she'd probably wear a tracksuit. Was that it? Was that why Ello was regarding her with such distaste?

Juliana decided to push past her daughter's contempt. "I have some news."

Ello went back to her eggs to demonstrate her lack of caring, and Ewan tried to slug his brother with a sippy cup. Garrett didn't even look up from his breakfast-based dinosaur project.

"Stop it, boys," Juliana commanded automatically. She uttered this phrase so often that she should put it on a T-shirt, on a bumper sticker, on her headstone. "Ello, do you want to hear?" she prodded, because the expression on Ello's face was so blank it wasn't even clear she understood the language her mother was using.

Garrett smashed his stegosaurus's head with a closed fist, sending a splatter of eggs over both boys.

"Sure," Ello admitted begrudgingly.

"It came over the parental portal this morning. They fixed the flood damage in the girls' locker room. So be sure to take your stuff today. Gym class is back on."

Ello had long ago mastered the dead stare, revealing nothing of the once-joyous little girl who Juliana fervently prayed still inhabited some part of her soul. Juliana assumed Ello liked gym class—who didn't?—so she wasn't expecting any particular reaction out of her daughter.

Instead, Ello rocked in her chair, widened her eyes, and took in a shocked breath. "No!" she wailed. "No. I can't. No. I can't. No."

Juliana was puzzled. "What do you mean, you can't? Can't what?"

"I mean I can't!" she shouted, leaping to her feet. "Nobody cares about me in this family. This is the worst day of my life!"

Ello ran from the room as if pursued by vampires, her mouth set in a silent scream. Juliana calmly poured herself a cup of coffee. Obviously, something huge was going on with Ello, something to do with gym class.

Juliana wondered what it could possibly be.

# CHAPTER TWO

J uliana was industriously cleaning Garrett's breakfast off of Ewan's face when her husband entered the kitchen.

"I just passed your daughter in the hallway," he declared.

"*My* daughter," Juliana repeated, so he knew she understood the significance. She stepped to the stove and began assembling Hunter's breakfast while he poured himself coffee, his agitation visible in the way he sloshed the black liquid into the cup and onto the counter.

"She's wearing more makeup than a beauty contestant," Hunter asserted heatedly, his message clear: *You're the mother. Do something. Prevent puberty.*

"Use the sponge on the counter," Juliana instructed him.

Hunter responded with a confused look—how was *that* what they were talking about?

Juliana nodded at the spill. "To soak that up," she elaborated helpfully.

"We can't let her go to school like that," Hunter insisted. "She'll get kicked out. We'll be charged with harboring a menace to society."

"No, she will not be kicked out," Juliana replied. She

gave up on trying to wipe Garrett's face completely clean and released him so that he could rocket off to join his brother in destroying whatever they were destroying that morning. "It's just lip gloss."

"She has eye black. And you can't see the freckles on her cheeks. She's pasted some kind of—of *paste* over them."

"All the girls in her grade look like that, Hunter. That's all they do, all day long, is put on makeup."

"Then how do they get it off their faces?" Hunter demanded. "With steel wool? A sandblaster? I don't think the fact that 'all the other girls look like that' is an excuse."

"You are laying down the law," Juliana observed.

Hunter stubbornly stuck his chin out.

"Drawing a line in the sand," she continued. "Coming back with your shield, or on it."

He threw up his hands. "Okay, what?"

Juliana set her husband's breakfast down in front of him with a tolerant expression. "I've learned to fight the battles that are important, Hunter, and otherwise just let things go. Ello won't always put on so much makeup, I promise. Right now, she wants to look exactly like every other girl in her grade. When she gets to high school and sees the older girls, she'll want to look like *them*."

He sighed. "I just miss our little girl. Isn't there some sort of pill we can give her so that she goes back to being how she was?" Hunter obviously meant to be kidding, but his face reflected real bewilderment that the child in bunny slippers who used to crawl in his lap for a story now acted as if everything about her father burned her like acid.

"If it makes you feel any better, she treats me even worse," Juliana informed him. "You get to escape to your job every day, while I'm stuck here with the twins, and when Ello gets home . . ." Juliana's words jammed in her throat. She hadn't meant to get started on *this*.

*Not yet.*

Ello stood in her room, leaning forward slightly, staring at her face in the mirror. She hated every single aspect of everything she saw. She had inherited her mother's Brazilian features, but without the extra melanin to have it all make sense. Instead, God's perverse joke had been to paint her skin in the same pale, soulless vanilla that her father's people had brought over with them on some boat from some place where everyone looked disgustingly the same.

Her distaste also applied to everything below her neck. *Especially* below the neck. She took in all her flaws, all of the intolerables that she dragged around with her, the Worst Body Ever, and turned away in disgust. This morning she had resentfully appraised her mother, who was still thin and sexy despite childbirth, making Ello feel like a walrus in comparison to the supermodel cooking breakfast. Her mom was *old*. It was So Unfair.

On the dresser beneath the mirror stood her trophies from ice dancing, which she had been doing since she was seven years old. In fifth grade, she had competed with other girls from all over the region and *won*, her father yelling and whistling as she glided out to accept her trophy. Then every other girl received the exact same trophy, which meant there was no point in trying hard at anything.

Ello reached for the drab, baggy sweater that had exemplified her style since before summer vacation. The shapeless garment draped her in featureless folds, exactly how she wanted. No one could see anything below her shoulders except her feet.

Not for the first time that week, or even that morning, Ello glanced at the framed photo montage that had replaced her unicorn poster a year ago. A birthday gift from her best friend, each photograph featuring only the two of them, Brittne and Ello, mostly selfies, all laughing, smiling, happy happy happy.

*Brittne.* She was the center of Ello's universe. The largest brown eyes of any human on the planet, perfect smile, hair blond and straight and flowing. Brittne's parents personified the word "average" in every apparent way, yet their daughter could silence a room by walking into it. At *thirteen*. But Brittne loved Ello and Ello loved her and the two were inseparable. Brittne was the only reason Ello was alive.

She turned back to the mirror. "Ugh," she pronounced, eloquently summing up how she felt about everything. How was she going to survive gym class?

Utter Disaster.

❋

Grunting because the thing was so heavy, Sander pulled the urn off the shelf in the bathroom closet. He kept it up so high to prevent the twins from taking it down and scattering their grandmother's ashes all over the living room.

Barbara was taking powerful occupation of his thoughts this morning—probably because of the chest pains in the night that had led him to believe he was having a heart attack, an event he viewed with ambivalence. He set the urn on the vanity and regarded the bright turquoise finish with irony. His wife had always loved southwestern-style jewelry, and would have been delighted, but she was inside it and he was outside, loathing how the color jammed a cheerful mood into a somber purpose. When they cremated Sander, they'd probably put his incinerated remains into a dull metal box, because that represented who he'd been ever since the light of his life was extinguished.

"I will see you again soon, darling," Sander whispered. He silenced his breathing, listening for a response from beyond the urn, but heard only the sound of Winstead scratching his ear.

Juliana sympathetically watched Hunter's stress crackle through him like an electric current, manifesting in the agitation with which he chopped up his scrambled eggs.

"So this is like the most important meeting of my whole career," he fretted. "Mrs. O'Brien and I haven't spoken much about the new installation, but now she wants a full briefing. Now. When we're, like, T-minus five."

Juliana assessed her husband. "And is that what you're wearing?" she asked blandly.

Hunter jerked his head up in alarm. "What? What do you mean?"

Juliana gave him a kind smile. "Maybe that tie doesn't go so well with that shirt," she suggested. "Let me get you something else."

"Have you seen where I put my coffee cup?" he asked.

Juliana walked to the counter and retrieved it. She took a breath, steeling herself. "And don't forget, we're having lunch today."

Well, he obviously *had* forgotten. He gave her a stricken look. "Oh."

Juliana shook her head. "This has been on the calendar for a long time, Hunter," she admonished. "We need to talk. It's important."

He stood and took his plate across the kitchen, setting it in the sink so that the housekeeping fairies could put it in the dishwasher for him. "I know," he agreed, though it was obvious he did *not* know, had not a clue what she wanted to talk about, "but it's just that this installation is running behind. This is huge, honey."

"I know," she responded. They said that to each other a lot, but did they "know"? Really?

Hunter absently set his coffee cup on the counter and left the room. Juliana waited patiently. After a minute or two, he poked his head back into the kitchen. "Did I leave my coffee in here?"

Juliana wordlessly handed him the cup, then turned to put his breakfast plate in the dishwasher. Her sigh was full and heavy. She'd prepared for this lunch the way she had once prepared for trial. Yet, despite her rehearsals, she felt filled with hesitation.

"How am I going to tell him?" she asked herself aloud.

The twins were in their car seats, kicking their legs and babbling to each other. Juliana glanced up at her children in the rearview mirror. Ello was peering out the window, either moody or pretending to be moody. Garrett couldn't manage to hit his brother with his tiny fist, so he threw a piece of cookie.

Ewan made an unintelligible remark, and the twins began laughing hilariously.

"What did he say?" Juliana asked her daughter, the translator.

"He said Garrett just peed his pants," Ello advised.

More raucous laughter.

"Well, did he?" Juliana asked.

"No way I'm checking *that*," Ello answered with a smile.

Juliana found herself marveling at how her daughter could go from being a wicked witch to a normal human being in seemingly no time at all. She decided not to mention it, for fear her daughter would transform back into The Creature Who Used To Be Normal.

Following the established routine, Juliana dropped Ello off at middle school first. Her daughter left the car with a slouch, telegraphing contempt. She made a beeline for the small, defensive cluster of almost-women chatting in front of the building.

"Those are the people," Juliana murmured, "my daughter prefers over her own family."

The leader of the pack had been Ello's best friend since first grade: Brittne. Juliana did not trust the girl, had never trusted her since the day Brittne's family moved into the house next door, back in their old neighborhood. When Juliana and Hunter bought their new house, Juliana had fantasized that Ello would make new friends, but all Ello ever talked about was Brittne.

The minivan dropped a wheel into a pothole with an artillery-level *bang*, startling the boys into silence. Juliana waited for the grinding vibration that would come with a blown tire. It didn't come, but now she was ultra alert. Her eyes took in the dead vegetation that marked Michigan in late November; she blinked at the low, scudding clouds while waiting patiently at a stoplight. In the summer, this intersection was backed up for a quarter of a mile, but once the autumn leaves were flushed from the trees, everyone with money and any sense fled the state.

Next stop: preschool. Juliana parked her car and wrestled her sons out of the grip of their car seats. "Ready for school?" she asked them in a singsong voice, holding their hands and guiding them into the building. There were days when the boys arched their backs and screamed as if she were leading them into Alcatraz. And then there were days like this, when as soon as they could yank their hands away, they ran to a pack of boys who were whacking each other with Styrofoam bats.

Finally, Juliana was free. She smiled as she exultantly steered her minivan toward the store. "This is your relaxation time, your 'me' time: a trip to Target," she announced to herself without irony.

Her minivan's video screen lit up with an incoming call: Mrs. Espinoza. Juliana stared at the display, her heart pounding.

"Oh no. . . ."

She couldn't let Mrs. Espinoza's call roll to voicemail, so she thumbed the button on her steering wheel.

"Hello?" she answered, trying to sift the dread from her voice.

"Mrs. Goss?" Mrs. Espinoza's voice inquired.

Though Mrs. Espinoza was from Honduras and Juliana was from Rio de Janeiro, and though they did not share a common language, Juliana had always felt that Mrs. Espinoza was her one secure ally in the world of tempers, timeouts, and laundry, laundry, laundry. But allies could be fickle, and Juliana always sensed that any ultimate betrayal would come in the form of a morning phone call from this woman.

Mrs. Espinoza was probably sick and wouldn't be able to work today. Or she had won the lotto, or her husband had gotten a transfer—something. It would be something.

"I am driving my brother's car," Mrs. Espinoza informed Juliana. "My own car broke. Do I need to register with the preschool?"

Juliana nearly sobbed with relief. "No, you'll be fine," she replied. "So, you can pick the twins up from their school today?"

"Oh, yes, as regular," Mrs. Espinoza assured her.

"Thank you. Thank you," Juliana all but gushed. She did not say it, but if Mrs. Espinoza had asked for a million dollars, Juliana would have found a way to get the money. Plain, unmarked bills. No cops.

They hung up. Juliana had her list for Target and knew she would blow through it quickly. "Plenty of time to make your lunch with Hunter," she told herself.

Her heart began pounding again.

# CHAPTER THREE

Winstead lay in his dog bed, a comfortable, pillow-based arrangement large enough for his huge, lanky frame. He had spent so much time lying in it that he could smell it as strongly as he could smell himself.

He had been aware of the house slowly draining of its occupants. First the man, Hunter, exited on a solo mission. Then the rest of everybody, a jumble of people-sounds as the mother, Juliana, herded her pack out into the garage. Then some mechanical noises, and then nothing.

Daddy sat slumped in his chair, a book slack in his hands, his mouth open, his chest barely rising and falling. Though Daddy did not seem to be able to sleep much during the night, in the day he often lapsed into these moments of slumber, a steady whispering sound escaping from between his teeth.

Winstead felt aches in his joints and knew that his person suffered from the same—it was evident in the involuntary groans and gasps Daddy emitted when struggling out of bed.

Winstead was concerned for Daddy. There had been a time when his person would take Winstead for walks around the block and actively play on the floor with him.

Then something happened to Mommy, who had been taking a lot of naps and was tended to by people who smelled of sharp chemicals. Winstead couldn't see her when it happened, but he registered Daddy's sharp cries and frantically scratched at the door of the room where Mommy had been shut in. Finally the door opened and Daddy came out, collapsed with him on the floor, and pressed a wet face into Winstead's fur. Whispering people slipped almost silently into the bedroom and later trundled Mommy's smell away on a high, rolling bed.

It was a day Winstead would never forget, a day he would never understand.

Shortly after that, Daddy and Winstead moved here, a house with two young boys who yelled a lot, a nice girl who sometimes petted him, and two adults who seemed too busy to pay much attention to a dog.

Winstead and Daddy had lived in the new, louder house long enough for two winters to pass, and another was approaching. Winstead did not understand why they didn't go back home, but Daddy was his everything, and as long as he was with Daddy, Winstead was happy, even though he knew Daddy was not. No matter how much Winstead loved his person, only Mommy could make Daddy happy. Often, as Winstead drifted off to sleep, he pictured Mommy at home, waiting for both of them to return.

Winstead inhaled, drawing in Daddy's scent. It was familiar, strong and sour. When they lived in the other place with Mommy, Winstead usually detected the soft fragrance of her bathroom items on Daddy's skin. Daddy was spending less and less time, though, getting wet and then dry in the bathroom. Less and less time doing anything at all. He was almost as motionless as Mommy had been toward the end.

Winstead's musings caused a quick uptick in his concern for his person. Ignoring the protest from his knee joints, he rose from his bed, stretched with a groan, padded over to Daddy, and put his head in his person's lap.

After a long internal struggle, Daddy finally opened his eyes. He seemed to search the room in confusion before settling his gaze on his dog. Winstead gave his tail a little wag.

"What is it, buddy?" Daddy asked. "You need to go out?"

Winstead knew what "go out" meant.

There was nothing the dog could do about it now; events had been set in motion. Daddy labored to his feet like a man weighed down by heavy blankets, finally setting his posture so that he could shuffle down the hallway. Winstead followed. Daddy proceeded to the sliding doors to the backyard and, grunting a little, wrestled one open. Cold air curled in, bringing fresh scents to Winstead's nose.

"Okay," Daddy urged, "go ahead."

Winstead reluctantly stepped out into the yard. The grasses were matted and dead. Vast amounts of leaves had fallen and been blown away by men with buzzing apparatuses, so the dry-leaf smell was less sharp than before. Winstead trotted over to a bush and lifted his leg, looking back toward the glass doors. This had worked before: a quick lift of the leg, and then Daddy would open the slider and Winstead could race back in.

Not today. Daddy was staring at the back fence, as if there were squirrels there, which there were not—that was the first thing Winstead had checked. And then Daddy turned away and was swallowed up by the deeper recesses of the house.

Winstead sat. He liked it out here in the backyard, but he loved it so much more when Daddy came out with him.

But Daddy never did.

*This is it,* Hunter announced dramatically to himself.

Would the suit impress Mrs. O'Brien? Juliana seemed to think so, but Hunter was dubious. His new boss was so hard to read. Thus far, he'd only interacted with her in the context of a larger meeting, with everyone there. The way she spent all of her time on sales and development told Hunter all he needed to know about her priorities. He had a multimillion-dollar redesign underway for the entire office, a project more than a year in the planning, and she'd never asked him a single thing about it.

But now they were about to have a face-to-face, prearranged, one-on-one exchange.

So many things could happen today. It could be, though the odds were against it, that Mrs. O'Brien would award Hunter the promotion he had been working so hard to secure. Maybe she wouldn't need to wait for the installation to be complete; she might be persuaded by the sheer magnificence of the plan he had electronically forwarded to her. Hunter had thought of everything and written it all down with color-coded priorities and dates. He knew that people regarded him as scatterbrained ("dreamy," Juliana insisted) but that was only in his personal life. His profession—managing what the four hundred employees probably thought of as the simple *givens* of an office building: the lights, supplies, elevators, admins—was plotted and documented and controlled. The company's recent hiring boom had meant constantly shifting and restacking and cramming until, finally, something had to give, and Hunter's proposal to refit the office with better, more space-efficient work surfaces had been approved because it was brilliant. His moving plan (a misnomer, because they were staying in the same place) proved he *deserved* that promotion. How could the company design, implement, and support their business software without him?

The soaring self-confidence deflated like a blown tire when he considered the alternative. So much was at stake with the moving plan that the meeting might be more along the lines of an indictment. Even if everything went smoothly—and what ever did?—he could still end up as the fall guy for a project that admittedly had gone a little over budget. Okay, a lot over budget.

That wasn't Hunter's fault. The previous boss, Mr. Park, had demanded a lot of fancy décor and installations that did nothing to add efficiency or value to the operation, although it did make it look as if Mr. Park were an important man running a successful company. That didn't matter now. The old boss was gone, Mrs. O'Brien was the new boss, and Hunter was the man straddling the two administrations with a set of decisions whose momentum could not be halted. The redesign was on track, and this train would either be a bullet or a wreck.

He stood for a moment outside Mrs. O'Brien's office. On her first day here, she'd declared that, unlike her predecessor, she had an "open-door policy."

As far as Hunter had observed, her door had been shut ever since.

He knocked and, upon summons, entered.

Hunter had practiced this moment in his mind. He needed to come in self-assured, uncowed, yet respectful of her position in the company. His plan had been to greet her with a cheerful, "Good morning, Mrs. O'Brien."

Instead he said, "You wanted to see me?"

*Lame.*

"Please come in and shut the door," Mrs. O'Brien suggested in an unreadable tone.

Hunter glanced around the office appraisingly. As was the case in nearly every executive office on this floor, Mrs. O'Brien's desk was backed by a large hutch. She had decorated it with photographs, mostly of a boy. Hunter tracked the timeline from baby-age to the most recent, in which the smiling child seemed to be about Hunter's daughter's age.

Mrs. O'Brien flashed a smile. "I don't know much about you, Hunter. I've been so busy trying to acquaint myself with the operations of our marketing and development processes that I simply haven't had time." She frowned. "The software engineers are not meeting their targets." A wave of a hand. "We'll talk about that in a minute. Meanwhile, why don't you tell me about yourself."

Hunter was ready for this one. "Well, I've lived here in Traverse City for ten years. I was the assistant facilities manager for Munson Medical Center. Then I worked as director of operations for a software start-up company that failed. I came here a little more than three years ago, and have been running facilities ever since."

Mrs. O'Brien nodded. "And?"

Hunter nodded as if he understood. "And," he repeated, "we've got this major installation. . . ."

Mrs. O'Brien shook her head. "I meant *and* as in, what else about you? I know that you're married. Do you have children?"

The questions sounded warm and personal, or at least intended to be warm and personal, but there was nothing in his boss's eyes that matched her words. They were dark and glittering as they coldly assessed Hunter in his impressive suit.

Hunter cleared his throat. "Oh, yes. My wife was a litigator for a small firm here in town. Then we had Ello—Eloise—and she was very sick, born premature, and it was a real struggle. So, my wife stayed home to be with our daughter."

"Good." Mrs. O'Brien nodded for him to continue.

"We wanted to have another child right away, but it was one of those things. Gosh, it's been three years ago now that the twins were born. Ewan and Garrett."

"Twins," Mrs. O'Brien observed. "That can't be easy. I

have only my son, Sean, who will be living with me now. He stayed back at his old school to finish out football season, and he'll be coming here over Thanksgiving. He's fourteen—a little old for eighth grade, they tell me, though that wasn't the case when we lived in Canada. He'll be attending your daughter's school, I imagine."

Hunter brightened. "You know what? I am sure my daughter would be happy to show Sean around school when he gets here."

Mrs. O'Brien smiled. "That would be lovely."

Hunter nodded. Done deal. He just had to remember. His hand twitched, as if to call his wife. Juliana was the rememberer of everything.

*Juliana.* He glanced surreptitiously at his watch. Still some time before he had to meet her for lunch. Noting something odd in her manner that morning, he had checked his calendar to make sure it wasn't their anniversary or a birthday or something. But no, just lunch. So why did he feel like he was in trouble, somehow?

"Well," Mrs. O'Brien said, her friendly smile turning off with an almost-audible click, "let's talk about this installation that I inherited from my predecessor. What can you tell me?"

Hunter felt a sinking sensation in his stomach. Had his boss not read any of the documentation he had so carefully prepared? Was he really here to explain, in the few minutes he had before he needed to leave, a plan so complicated that he himself could hardly keep it all in his head?

The "inherited from my predecessor" was a clear signal

that he didn't have her support. What he needed to do was completely win her over, because if she rejected his underlying concepts, he was doomed.

But that would take time—time he didn't have before meeting Juliana.

# CHAPTER FOUR

Hunter obviously couldn't tell his boss he needed to cut the meeting short because of lunch with his wife, but as he began speaking, his stomach lurched as if he were falling off of a building—as if he were doing something really wrong to Juliana. Mentally, he shook it off. *Time to focus. High stakes.*

"So," he began, "research indicates that the reason so many software companies like ours have problems is because in today's world, the engineers and other critical players don't ever speak to each other. They email, they text, but they don't talk."

Mrs. O'Brien nodded. "Aware," she replied curtly.

"Okay." He registered her blunt reply as a bad omen, but plunged ahead regardless. "So, Thanksgiving Thursday and the following three days, we'll move all of the furniture out of the building and install new workstations, paint the walls, all that. When everyone returns Monday morning, they'll find a highly collaborative environment with desks that flow into worktables. To have a meeting, all they need to do is swivel their chairs around and scoot up to the common table. We have pop-up conference rooms that can be folded back into the wall so that at any moment a team can have privacy from others while they work together to solve problems. Every company that's tried this approach has reported much greater team efficiency and better quality control."

Hunter had to make a conscious effort not to appear proud as he sat back in his chair. He stole a quick look at his wristwatch.

Mrs. O'Brien nodded, looking . . . what . . . bored? Hunter suspected she had read his detailed plan after all.

"I'm sure you are aware that this isn't just our headquarters," she said. "It's our showcase facility. Our branch offices have sales meetings and presentations as well, but this is where the big boys fly in from the Fortune 500 firms. I am more than looking forward to getting rid of this tacky furniture." She gestured dismissively to the hutch where her photographs were displayed.

Hunter nodded as if he agreed with this assessment, though to him the towering shelves behind her were actually quite nice. He had wanted to keep the executive offices unchanged, saving hundreds of thousands of dollars, but Mr. Park had insisted on redoing every setup with much more luxurious furniture, regardless of cost. Given Mrs. O'Brien's stated disdain for the current installation, Hunter was thankful Mr. Park had been so self-indulgent—Mrs. O'Brien would find her new furniture far from "tacky."

"And you've managed to sell this junk?" Mrs. O'Brien asked, gesturing again at the shelves. "I saw the emails."

Hunter nodded eagerly. "Yes—there's almost no market for used office furniture, but I managed to secure a deal with a start-up in town to buy our executive setups. Everything else goes to a wholesaler, who's giving us a fair price." He glanced again at his watch.

"All right." Mrs. O'Brien reached for a pad, picked up a pen, and wrote something on it. Probably, *I'm making him late for his lunch.* "I'm sure you know that if this is successful, and indeed increases productivity at the levels you've guaranteed, we'll want to proceed with similar installations across the whole company. Every location."

Hunter had to restrain himself from wincing at the word "guaranteed." How could anyone guarantee anything?

"You would be the natural person for the job. It would be a new position in the company—instead of facilities manager for this location, you would be the director of corporate facilities," she continued, watching him steadily.

Hunter nodded neutrally, though inside he was uncorking champagne.

Mrs. O'Brien pursed her lips. "And I suppose it has to be said: this installation and its over-budget cost was not my doing. Mr. Parks is gone, of course, but you are not gone, and your name is all over everything." Mrs. O'Brien gave Hunter a frank and somewhat hostile gaze. "I am a bottom-line leader and, bottom line, if this fails, we will not require your services at our company any longer."

When Ello shut her locker, Soffea was right there, smiling blandly.

Grade school had been ruled by the three of them: Soffea, Ello, Brittne. When Ello had moved to her new house, though, she no longer lived a few steps away from her friends' homes. Ello's friendship with Brittne had survived intact, but somehow Soffea kept falling farther and farther out of the circle, as if she were on a boat that was slowly drifting away from shore.

Soffea had also missed the memo that eighth grade was supposed to be about forming fleeting, collapsing alliances with different malevolent factions, knives out and backs stabbed, the gossip quick with judgment. Soffea somehow sailed through life unperturbed, oblivious to all of it. Pretty much the opposite of Brittne.

"Have you seen her?" Ello asked, as if Soffea could read her mind. "Brittne, I mean. She didn't answer my text."

"She's around," Soffea answered with a shrug.

"Okay." Ello glanced up and down the halls but couldn't spot Brittne anywhere.

"Glad we'll finally be back in gym class," Soffea announced mildly. "About time."

Ello stared. Why would Soffea mention *that*? Did she *know*? Ello had two more hours before gym class and then her Life Was Over.

"Well," Soffea said, signing off with her trademark unbothered expression, "see you later."

Ello turned, trudging to her first class. Soffea's reminder had punched solid holes in Ello's denial. Gym class was going to happen. Ello could not pretend otherwise.

To make everything perfect, perfect, on this Perfectly

Awful Day, Brittne flowed across the hall, seemingly oblivious to the boys who tracked her every movement with haunted expressions. That's what her thick, shiny blond hair and her high cheekbones and gloriously large, dark brown eyes did to people.

"So," Brittne greeted her. "What did *she* want?"

*She.* The model-thin Brittne evidently held their childhood friend in utter contempt now, and Ello had a sick feeling she knew why.

"I guess we have gym class today," Ello replied faintly.

"I guess," Brittne agreed.

As if it were no big deal at all.

Hunter was technically not *that* late, except that it took him eight minutes to find a place to park and another five to hoof it to the restaurant. Of course, Juliana was already seated and reading the menu. She had probably arrived early and was mentally subtracting ten points for every minute he was delayed. By his calculations, Hunter was down about seventy billion points so far in this marriage.

"Hey, honey," he greeted her, a bit breathless. "So, so sorry I'm late. I thought I had plenty of time, but then traffic . . ."

She was waving off his apology. "Didn't you wear an overcoat this morning?" she asked, frowning. Hunter looked blankly down at his sport coat. No wonder he'd been so cold as he hustled down the sidewalk.

"Oh, yeah. I must have left it hanging on the hook in my

office." He took his seat. "Honestly, I thought you'd be more angry I left you waiting."

Her return look was challenging. "Is that how you see me? Angry for no reason?"

"Well, no," he fumbled, though it seemed that she was always irritated by normal male behavior. "I just know you don't like to be kept waiting." There; that seemed like a safe explanation. Hunter looked around the restaurant. He wasn't much interested in the aesthetics of design; he hired professionals to match colors and pick out artwork for his facility. But he was intrigued by the layout of any place where furniture could enhance or inhibit efficiency. This restaurant seemed to lean toward the latter, with so many tables jammed into the tight space that they impeded the ability of a server to navigate them. Hunter started to calculate the trade-off between a) having more places to seat more customers, and b) restricted access, resulting in slower service, so that table turnover took longer.

"What are you thinking?" Juliana asked.

Hunter blinked at her, not sure he knew the answer to that. "Oh," was his response.

Juliana nodded as if this were an actual answer. Hunter decided he'd better run to safe ground.

"I really admire how organized you are," he told her. He was utterly sincere—she was his Atlas, and if she shrugged, the whole family would tumble into an abyss. "It's why you were such a good trial attorney."

Her eyes flashed. "Were?" she repeated.

"What? No. I mean, you're an excellent trial attorney. *Are*. You're amazing, Juliana."

*How many more feet can I stick in my mouth?*

He watched as some sort of dismal change came over his wife, something he'd observed more than once recently in her posture, often at breakfast, as if his Atlas were indeed growing weary of the world on her shoulders.

"No, you're right," Juliana admitted with a sigh. "You either are a trial attorney, or you *were* a trial attorney. I haven't had that job since I got pregnant with Eloise."

Hunter kept a watchful eye on his wife while they ordered lunch. Something was going on that he did not understand. For reasons he didn't comprehend, his pulse rate had increased. He took a long pull on his iced tea. "Well, hey, I had my meeting with Mrs. O'Brien," he informed her. "She seemed really excited about the installation project." *If 'excited' is a synonym for 'threatening.'* "If it goes well, I mean really well, I'd be put in charge of all facilities company-wide. Promotion."

Juliana regarded him with an unreadable expression. "So it's for sure that you would take the job," she stated carefully.

"Well, yeah." Hunter shifted in his chair. Once again, a sense of imminent danger rose within him. "We talked about it, remember?"

"Yes," she agreed evenly, "we discussed it. We said there were many variables. You also told me it would mean a lot of travel."

"Right, well, we have twenty branches in the United States and four up in Canada. They're small operations, some of them no more than five or six people, but all facilities share the same characteristics." Hunter leaned forward excitedly. "For example, I've always wanted us to order all of our supplies as a national account so that we could accrue savings across our locations. Currently, though, each individual office manager . . ." Hunter's enthusiastic gush trailed off, halted by the unhappy shape of Juliana's mouth.

A long silence followed.

"What is it?" he asked.

Juliana looked away from his gaze. Hunter's nagging fear bloomed into full-on panic. This was Juliana Oliveira, a woman who was never anything but blunt and up-front. He had never seen her avoid his eyes before. His heart was pounding again, and he could almost predict the next words that came out of her mouth.

"Hunter," she sighed softly. "I'm just not happy in our marriage."

# CHAPTER FIVE

Ello stood and stared at her gym locker as if fasci-
nated. The school administrators had taken advantage of the repairs necessitated by a broken pipe
to change the gym's décor. Now the metal lockers were
sprayed a pastel yellow, and the walls were pastel blue with
pastel green accents, as if they lived in Florida and not a
state where all liquid water spent half the year frozen as
hard as rock. Around her, classmates were struggling into
their workout clothes, feeling awkward and unfamiliar after having gone more than a year without regular physical
education classes.

Well, This Was It.

Ello seized the hem of her draping, baggy sweater and
lifted it over her head in one quick motion, revealing her
sports bra, not looking left, not looking right.

She heard an inhalation. Not a gasp, but definitely an
involuntary intake of air. And, as ridiculous as it seemed
to recognize someone by her *breathing*, Ello knew exactly
who had pulled in a lungful of shocked oxygen.

It was, of course, Brittne.

Ello deliberately did not look at her best friend. Did not

so much as glance at what she knew would be an expression that could Literally Kill.

In Brittne's mind, Ello was guilty of a betrayal, of maturing past Brittne in a time and a place and a clique where such changes were anything but welcome. Next year, maybe, high school, everything would be fine again. But in eighth grade, for now, in Brittne's circle of devotees, it was a *curse*.

When Ello finally turned away from the locker, Brittne was gone.

Her husband watched in stunned silence as Juliana reached into her purse, pulled out a small spiral notebook, and opened it to a numbered series of entries on the page.

"You have a list?" he demanded. "A list of everything wrong with our relationship? With me as a husband?"

Juliana pressed her lips together. This was as hard as she had imagined it would be. The hurt, the fear, and the shock in Hunter's eyes completely unnerved her. She wanted nothing more right then than to put the list away and tell him it was all a misunderstanding. But that wasn't how Juliana operated—she made a plan and stuck to it.

"These are just some things I wanted to talk to you about and was afraid I'd forget," she corrected reassuringly. "Just listen, okay?"

Hunter gave a faint nod, staring at her like a man watching his firing squad line up.

Juliana looked at the first item on her list and pulled in a deep breath. "I know I'm not supposed to say this, but the twins are the worst thing that has ever happened in my life."

When picturing herself saying this to him, Juliana had imagined that she and Hunter would share a laugh of rueful acknowledgment. Instead, he continued to stare silently. It made her not want to look at him. She plunged on. "And our daughter, in case you haven't noticed, has become a full-on, no-holds-barred teenager. She goes into sullen silences or screaming rages without any warning at all. I need you to back me up when I lay down the law with her, because she's been doing an end run to you whenever I give her an answer she doesn't like."

"Are you thinking of leaving me?" Hunter asked plaintively. "Divorce?"

*God.* Juliana shook her head. "No, no, that's not it. I *love* you, Hunter. I just kind of hate my life right now."

"Well, how about if Mrs. Espinoza comes more than three times a week? She could pick up the twins after preschool every single day, maybe, and then she could keep them an hour longer?"

"That's not the essential problem," Juliana replied. "You've been absent so much. The kids need a father, and I need my life partner. Remember when we first got married? We were both working so hard, and yet somehow it seemed like we spent more time together then, when I was with the firm and you had that job at the hospital. And then there's your dad. . . . He doesn't do anything at all to help. He just sits in his room. We serve him food, we clean up after him, he never says thank you, and he's depressed— clinically depressed—but refuses to seek help."

From his expression, Juliana could tell that Hunter had swung into problem-solving mode.

"Okay," he responded eagerly, "what if you go back to work, like, part-time?"

Juliana was already shaking her head. "Oh, there's nothing I want more in the world than to go back to my old job, but there *is* no 'part-time' for a trial attorney, Hunter. It's impossible."

Hunter was processing a list of his own. "I'll talk to my father, I really will. And, once this big project is over, my schedule will calm down. . . ."

"Honey, you have not worked fewer than sixty hours a week since you took the job. And now you're going to be promoted and start leaving town?"

"So are you saying that if I get the promotion, I should turn it down?"

Juliana could see that the concept was completely foreign to him. But if he worked on the road for days on end, how would she be any different from a single mom?

"It's something I've worked for my whole career," he argued. "It's the game-changer we've both been waiting for, a way to get ahead financially. A way to make everything right."

"Hunter," Juliana replied softly, "how would you leaving town on a regular basis make everything *right*?"

"I'm sorry. . . . I didn't know you were feeling this way. I . . ." Hunter spread his hands out helplessly, truly gobsmacked. Then his eyes widened in horror. "Is there someone else?"

"What?" Juliana cried, then lowered her voice. "*No*. Stop making this into such a catastrophe. Couples have conversations like this with each other all the time. Honey, I feel like I'm drowning. I'm just asking for help."

Hunter's expression said it all—he had no idea what to do.

Sander stood in his bathroom, alone in the house, alone in his life. In front of him, lined up like soldiers, were orange plastic bottles with white lids, each a medication prescribed for recent health issues. Vicodin for when he blew out his back: maybe eight of those left. Valium for after Barbara died: only a few rattling around in the bottom of the pill bottle. Ambien to help him sleep, though eventually he'd realized it was addictive and had stopped taking it.

All in all, a hefty handful of tablets. Would it be enough to do the job?

Sander had also stumbled upon another medication while looking for something else in another bathroom: a packet of citalopram, an antidepressant Juliana was apparently taking clandestinely. What if he added those to the mix? Probably that would do it, but he hated to think about how guilty his daughter-in-law would feel.

Sander turned at a slight and familiar noise. Winstead had eased out of his dog bed, padded over, and was now standing in the doorway of the bathroom, regarding Sander with those old, soulful eyes.

"Hey there, Winstead," Sander greeted softly.

He stared at his dog, who stared back. It felt as if his brain were processing something deep in his subconscious, a background calculation. It would be easier to swallow the pills without thinking about what he was doing. Just get it done.

He pictured Winstead watching loyally, escorting his person out of the mortal world. Sander would do it in his chair, he decided, so that his hand could rest on Winstead's head. Leave this life touching his best friend. Or maybe call the dog up on the bed, lie on his back with Winstead's head on his chest, his arm draped over the wolfhound.

When he slipped away, would Winstead know it? His body would go silent. He pictured his dog nosing him in concern, trying to wake him up, growing more and more panicked. He'd whimper; he'd lick Sander's face; he'd cry out loud, pleading for a human to come help.

But by then, Sander would be beyond help.

The thought made Sander shudder. He wasn't ready, not yet. His knees popped as he knelt in front of his dog. He reached out and seized Winstead's head with both hands. "Okay, buddy," Sander said huskily. "Not today."

When Sander lowered his face to Winstead's, the dog

swiped his cheek with his tongue. It broke him, that doggy kiss, it broke Sander, and he gathered his best friend into his arms and sobbed into his dog's wiry fur.

The next morning, Juliana was at the stove. She liked to cook. When the mood struck her, she would prepare *feijoada*, her mother's black bean and pork stew, or her favorite: rich, delicious *pão de queijo*—Brazilian cheese bread. Hunter showed his appreciation for such efforts by patting his stomach, an unconscious gesture Juliana found charming. Sander didn't comment, but he always finished whatever Juliana placed in front of him. Her three children turned away from such preparations as if the food had spent a week lying dead in the road.

*Sander*. Juliana had learned exactly how he preferred his fried eggs, and making them had become so automatic that she executed the steps in precise order, always perfectly, never making them for anyone else in the family. The secret was basting them right before they were done. Normally she went through the motions without complaint, but this morning it irritated her, like everything irritated her these days.

She heard Hunter step into the kitchen earlier than the regularly scheduled program. "I'll take Dad his breakfast," he announced, his tone of voice sounding like he was saying, "I will now enter the burning building and save some orphans, plus establish a scholarship fund for them."

He took the tray as Juliana expertly dropped bacon next to the perfect eggs and the perfect toast.

"He doesn't understand a thing you told him," Juliana murmured to herself after he left.

"What?" Ello asked as she arrived.

"Just talking to myself, honey," Juliana replied.

"You say that like it's normal. But you're the only person who does it, Mom," Ello accused her. She moved to grab Sander's tray, then peered at Juliana in confusion.

"Your dad took Grandpa his breakfast," Juliana advised.

Ello's eyes bulged as if Juliana had announced that their father had just given live birth. She recovered quickly, though, sitting at the table and pulling out her phone. "Okay, Mom, we should get a dog," Ello announced. "I made a list of reasons why."

"Oh, honey."

Her daughter's eyes flashed. "Would you just listen to me for once? I don't have any friends! I need a dog!"

Juliana shook her head. "This isn't a good time."

Ello looked up sharply at her. "What's going on?"

"What do you mean?"

"Are you and Dad getting a divorce?"

The question made Juliana light-headed. What sort of subliminal messages had she been sending her daughter? Why did both Hunter and Ello go there so automatically, so effortlessly, when to Juliana the word sounded more like a fatal disease? *Divorce.*

"Oh, honey," she said again.

Ello kept staring, her eyes full of burning accusation.

Juliana glanced away, almost ill. Was that really what she wanted?

# CHAPTER SIX

Sander glanced up in surprise when his door pushed open without warning and his son stood there with his breakfast.

"What happened, is Ello sick?" Sander asked by way of greeting.

"Uh . . ." was Hunter's response, an answer Sander found lacking in specificity.

Since Hunter had never brought breakfast, he didn't know where to set the tray. He stood, frowning, obviously considering the options from a facilities-management point of view. The small table by the window was stacked with books and magazines. There was a tray for eating in bed, but Sander was up and dressed.

"Right here," Sander suggested mercifully, indicating the table next to his chair.

Hunter set the breakfast down. Sander eyed his food with no enthusiasm. Winstead lifted his nose for the bacon.

"Ello's fine. I just wanted to do it this morning." Hunter settled into a different chair, a serious expression on his face.

Ello never did this, never hung around for prolonged conversation, and Sander decided that's how he preferred it—drop breakfast and flee like a zookeeper feeding grizzly bears.

"How are you doing, really?" Hunter asked.

Sander frowned at the way his son posed the question. "What do you mean, *really*?"

"I just . . . I worry a little bit, Dad. You don't seem to do anything. You never take Winstead for a walk. You just sit in your room. We serve you food, we clean up after you. It's like you're depressed."

Winstead became alert when the word "walk" was spoken in association with his name, but opted not to get out of his bed in case Hunter was bluffing.

"Do? What do you want me to do?" Sander asked irritably.

"Well, what about finishing the restoration of your car?" Hunter proposed reasonably. "You completely stopped working on it when Mom died. Weren't you going to put a new engine into it?"

Sander grunted. "Don't got one."

Hunter nodded. "Yeah, I know, I was online looking at companies that specifically specialize in classic car engines. I found one for a 1981 Monte Carlo that—"

"—1980," Sander cut in. The conversation was making him itchy.

"Oh, sorry. Well, I'm sure they have those too."

Sander shook his head. "I don't trust the Internet."

Hunter didn't have anything to say to that.

As Sander regarded his son, the intense expression in Hunter's eyes made him turn away.

*Pity.* Sander could have endured concern, but this wasn't that.

This was pity.

Hunter returned to the kitchen, peering around as if searching for flaws. "Anyone seen my coffee cup?"

"You set it on the counter there when you took your dad his tray," Juliana told him.

Hunter grabbed the cup, sipped, found it tepid, and put it in the microwave. While waiting, he slapped his hands together in an, "Okay what's next?" gesture. "How else can I help, Juliana?"

His wife gave him a tolerant smile and he couldn't help but grin back. Okay, she was right: he was not going to fix everything that was bothering her with one hyper-efficient morning, but it was a start, right? Everything ever done began with a start.

"Here's something," Juliana offered. "You could locate the twins. They ran by a few minutes ago headed toward the back of the house. It was weird . . . they weren't yelling or holding anything that could be used as a weapon."

Hunter nodded and turned to his daughter. "Did you see where the boys went?"

"Oh," Ello responded scornfully. "I get it. Your way of finding the twins is to ask me to do it for you."

In that moment, as his little girl glared at him, Hunter was struck by how much she resembled her mother. True, her hair was his, a light brown that she'd been begging for years to be allowed to dye blond, something Hunter had decreed wouldn't be allowed until she no longer wanted it. Ello's eyes were all Hunter and Sander, too—green, a fleck or two of black floating in them, which Ello considered hideous imperfections. She even sported a few faint freckles. They were the first things to go when she began troweling on makeup. But her high cheekbones, the broad smile (so seldom on display, recently), dark brows, and the intriguing pucker between her nose and her full lips—those were pure Juliana. Ello would someday be as beautiful as her mother. At that point, all boys would be prohibited.

"I see your point," Hunter responded affably. Ello's eyes widened at her father's decision to speak to her like an adult. "All right," he announced, "this can't be too hard. I'll just follow the sound of things breaking."

Hunter did not have far to go. At the end of a hallway was a closet where they stored goods purchased at Costco. They probably had five hundred dollars locked up in toilet paper, but they'd saved at least a nickel a roll. The door to this home warehouse was kept firmly latched with a knob that, as far as common wisdom held, was too stiff for little boys' hands to turn. But the door was cracked ajar. Hunter flung it open and, because the situation called for it, cried, "A-*ha*!"

The boys reacted to the ambush by giggling. They had managed to rip open a bag full of chocolate chip cookies and, judging by the crumbs on their shirts, had consumed seven pounds apiece.

"All right, gentlemen," Hunter announced in a stern voice. "Go back to the kitchen. Those cookies rightfully belong to me."

The twins glanced at each other and indulged in brief, unintelligible conversation.

"Ello isn't here to translate, so I'll take that as a 'yes, sir.' Now let's go." Hunter walked behind them like a court officer. Back in the kitchen, he put the boys in their high chairs. He felt almost euphoric—he could *do* this. Juliana wouldn't be unhappy with him for long.

"Where'd you find them?" she queried.

"They were having breakfast," Hunter replied. "Has anyone seen my coffee cup?"

Juliana gestured with a spatula toward the microwave, which chirped helpfully.

"Right." He opened the door and put his hand on the cup. The coffee was back to being cold. He shut the door and punched the microwave back on.

"Mom and I were just talking about maybe we should get a dog," Ello stated forcefully. She was eyeing her father with such an odd intensity that he turned and shot a baffled glance at Juliana.

Juliana communicated something with her dark eyes, a warning, and Hunter figured he knew what it meant. A new dog would only be another burden on his wife, who was already at a breaking point. *Unhappy in our marriage.* He started shaking his head. "Oh, no, wow, this would not be a good time for a new dog," he advised, happy he could back up Juliana on this.

The way his wife and Ello both stared at him suggested he had just committed a colossal blunder. What was going on? He decided to try again. "What about Winstead? We already have a dog."

"Winstead's old," Ello said scornfully.

Ewan proclaimed something like, "Ah Wensaw we go eh fart!" He and his brother found this impossibly hilarious.

"He said all Winstead ever does is fart," Ello translated.

Hunter nodded. "Thank you. How nice that Ewan's first intelligible word was 'fart.'"

The boys reacted to their father's statement like drunks at a comedy club, convulsing with laughter.

Juliana sighed.

"So, hey, I'm doing chauffeur duty this morning," Hunter announced, looking for his coffee cup.

"Oh my God," Ello groaned. "This will be the absolute worst."

Ello was so sullenly silent in the car that it made Hunter want to turn and yell at her. He asked her about her classes and got a grunt. He asked her about her friends and received the same response. The twins were behind them, chattering to each other in their alien tongue, and all Hunter wanted was . . . Well, what he wanted might be impossible. He simply wanted his daughter to *like* him again.

He brightened. "Hey, Ello. My boss has a son a little older than you in your grade."

Ello reacted not at all to this announcement.

"I guess he's been living with his father until the end of football season. Now he's moving here and will be going to your middle school. I told my boss you'd be happy to show the guy around."

Finally, a response. Ello jolted as if she had just taken a direct hit. "*What?*" she replied in a scream that would've satisfied the director of any horror movie.

"Yeah," Hunter continued reasonably. "He'll be here the Monday after Thanksgiving. We'll pick him up and take him to school and you can introduce him to your friends. His name is Sean."

"Oh my God, Dad, you are ruining my life!" Ello shrieked, her face contorted as if she were being hit with jolts of electricity.

"I don't get it," Hunter said, because he did not get it. "What's the big deal?"

"The big deal?" Ello demanded. "Don't you think my life is hard enough already? Do you know what I'm going through? Don't you understand that my generation has a harder time than any other generation in the history of the world?"

Hunter let that proclamation echo around the car for a second or two, savoring the concept. "Really," he observed. "So, the kids growing up in the Great Depression? Or how about if you lived in Germany during Hitler? Or if you grew up under Pol Pot? Do they even teach Pol Pot at school, or do you think I'm talking about some sort of cooking device?"

Hunter dropped his self-congratulatory grin when he saw Ello glaring at him. "Okay," he offered reasonably, "why don't you name some ways that your generation has it worse than any other generation in the history of the world, including the people in the Spanish Inquisition."

Ello's expression turned smug. "That's simple. Cell phones."

Hunter drove. He nodded. Silence sat with them in the car. He nodded some more. "You know what? That answer is so perfect I really just want to take some time to think about it."

Ello saw Brittne speaking to Mourgen and marched up to the two of them, her face set in righteous indignation.

"You know what my dad just told me? Some new guy, some ozay kid from, like, Detroit, is moving here and my dad says I got to take him around school like I'm a seeing-eye dog or something, and I'm, like, gonna be stuck with this dweeby dude and he'll probably think I'm his best friend, and then it will be impossible to get rid of him."

This was the sort of scandal that attracted Brittne the way blowflies swarmed to a corpse. Ello waited expectantly for feigned horror, knowing Brittne would find the whole thing delicious. That's who Brittne was. Gossip was her *raison d'être*. You put up with it because she was the richest, most beautiful, most popular girl in the school, and Ello's Best Friend For Life.

But Brittne surprised Ello by not reacting much at all. She gave a slight uplift of her perfectly plucked eyebrow to indicate she had heard, but otherwise—nothing.

Mourgen sniffed. "Boring," she pronounced.

Ello regarded Mourgen uncertainly, not sure why she was even *here*. Mourgen so obviously adored Brittne, wanted to be Brittne, that Brittne had shunned her for, like, ever, just (as far as Ello could tell) so Brittne could revel in the Power Of Brittne. The school had one queen and she decided who was in and who was out. Had Mourgen somehow been resurrected?

Ello turned to Brittne, trying to get a read on the situation, but the bland, contemptuous expression in her best friend's eyes drained her of strength. Ello walked away with a nauseating clinch in her stomach, unsteadily heading back to her locker, feeling every eye in eighth grade watching her.

Something very bad was happening.

# CHAPTER SEVEN

Winstead understood the significance of Daddy closing his book with a dry *clap*: it signaled that something was going to happen now. The dog decided to feign sleep—he was not in the mood to go back out into the yard. He heard the chair squeak as Daddy struggled up into a standing position, grunted, took a deep breath, let it out slowly.

"Hey, buddy, are you asleep?"

Winstead did not understand the question but didn't hear anything promising a treat or a meal, so he remained motionless, eyes lidded.

"Come on, big guy. Let's go out to the garage."

Winstead couldn't help himself; he raised his head as his person shuffled across the room, then jumped out of his dog bed when he heard the bedroom door open. His curiosity was simply irresistible, even though he was almost certain that Daddy was heading for the sliding doors to the backyard. Winstead would gladly go anywhere, but he wanted it to be with Daddy.

To Winstead's surprise, the backyard was not the destination. Daddy moved through the kitchen and to the garage.

Winstead stepped briskly now, eager to explore the exotic scents out there.

The lights came on and Daddy shut the door behind them. Winstead began sniffing around the base of the trash cans, turning when Daddy started pulling on a heavy canvas that made a loud rustling noise. As soon as the tarpaulin hit the floor, an odor, long familiar and musty, filled Winstead's nostrils. He trotted over to the car and sat before the door expectantly.

For a long time, his person did nothing but just stand there. Finally, though, the car door opened and Winstead immediately bounded onto his place in the back seat. He settled his head on the doorframe. Sometimes there was a roof on this car, and sometimes there wasn't. Right now, there wasn't.

Daddy settled in behind the steering wheel and closed the door. "I could do that. . . . I could put a new engine in her," he remarked. "Get her driving again."

Winstead did not hear a single word he recognized. He sighed, looking forward to getting rolling. He had so many marvelous memories of this car. Car rides with Mommy and Daddy, the top open to the sky, exotic smells whistling into his muzzle at a provocative velocity. Sometimes Mommy would reach out and touch Daddy's shoulder with a light hand. The gesture always made Winstead wag.

Most of the best smells had surrendered their hold on the interior air of the car. But Winstead could still sense Mommy, her scent worked into the leather seats and other gathered, tight places. Faint, yes, but Mommy was still here in this car.

Daddy said a few words, almost mumbling, and Winstead knew they were not directed at him. Not dog words. Perhaps Daddy was talking to Mommy because he smelled her too.

Winstead sighed, ready to get moving. He loved Daddy and he loved car rides.

And so he waited.

Hunter felt a flash of guilt as palpable as a sudden sweat when Juliana asked him if he had noticed that she'd decorated the home for Thanksgiving . . . because of course he hadn't. He looked around wildly, and yes, the signs of the upcoming holiday were everywhere, from the turkey ornaments to the basket of orange gourds to the art-class sign that said WE GIVE THANKS, created by (third-grade) Ello out of what looked to be toothpaste on a piece of driftwood.

"Very pretty," Hunter replied, knowing this wasn't exactly an answer to her question.

"Is Sander coming out for dinner?" Juliana asked.

Hunter turned to his daughter. "Did you tell him about dinner?"

Ello nodded. "I told him, plus Garrett threw a plastic tomahawk into his room and I think it hit him."

"Seems like sufficient notice," Hunter observed.

"It was from the box of Thanksgiving decorations," Ello continued. "The tomahawk symbolizes our oppression of native peoples. If there were any justice, we would all go back where we came from and leave the country to the people who were here first."

"Okay," Hunter agreed, "we'll leave after dinner." Ello gave him a dark, fuming glare as he stood up. "I'll go talk to Dad."

Hunter found his father watching television. Winstead was sprawled in his dog bed and didn't react to Hunter's arrival. "Hey, Dad. Are you coming to dinner?"

Sander aimed his remote at the television and snapped off his program with an odd sort of viciousness. "Can I just eat in here?" he demanded in a surly tone.

"Why?"

"The twins drive me crazy."

"Of course, that's what they're for, to drive us crazy."

Sander heaved a sigh, and a moment later Winstead followed suit. Hunter regarded his father for a long moment. "Hey, Dad, do you mind if I ask you a personal question?" he asked, surprising himself.

Sander addressed the query with a look that was neither inviting nor discouraging.

"Did you and Mom ever . . ." Hunter abandoned the sentence and started over. "I'm really worried that Juliana is thinking of leaving me."

Sander stared at him as if he were speaking the language of the twins.

"She says she's not happy," Hunter continued, afflicted with the sudden urge to sob. He took a breath to tamp it down. "With the marriage, I mean. Except, when she talks, it seems like it's really less the marriage than everything else. Like, the twins, and you, and just everything. I mean, she was a high-powered attorney, and now all she does is take care of dependent organisms. Of which I am one, right? But I have to work, and we have the twins. That's not something I can change. But maybe she's so fed up she's just thinking the hell with it, she'd rather not be married."

His father's expression remained maddeningly opaque.

"She wants to go back to work, she said. More than anything, she said. And then she said our current situation makes that impossible. I don't know what to do," Hunter confessed into the void.

Winstead sighed again. Hunter waited.

"Well," Sander said at last, "what can you do? If she's unhappy, she'll leave."

Hunter gazed at his father in disbelief. After a moment, he turned away. "Tell you what," he tossed over his shoulder, "we'll make a plate for you, and you come get it whenever you want. I really don't care."

Hunter rejoined his family. Juliana gave him a questioning look and he shrugged in reply. No words were necessary; her question and his answer were clear to both of them. Ewan said something and Garrett, giggling, seized a handful of Jell-O and squished it. Juliana reached out with a wet kitchen towel and expertly wiped away the gooey mess, moving from the boy's fingers to his face. Sputtering,

Garrett tried to escape what Hunter admired as effective negative reinforcement.

"Next time, maybe keep your hands off your food," Hunter advised his son.

"Ewan told him to do it," Ello volunteered.

"So, hey," Hunter said to his daughter, "how was school today?"

It seemed an innocuous, routine question. But Ello's face turned dark and she stared grimly at her plate. Hunter resisted the urge to order her to look at him. "Ello?" he prodded, with what he felt was benign patience.

"Brittne hates me," Ello mumbled into her mashed potatoes.

Time for another husband-and-wife glance. Hunter's position on Brittne had always been that she was an incurable affliction on his family. Being rid of Brittne meant, to him, that they should open champagne or bat a pinata. Hunter mulled over his response, finally deciding on, "Why do you say that?"

Ello continued to focus on her carbohydrates.

"Ello?" he prompted after a moment.

"I don't want to talk about it!" she seethed, lasering him with a searing glare.

Hunter directed a glance at his wife that was equal parts helplessness and accusation. Ello had morphed into this sullen creature on Juliana's watch; ergo, Juliana needed to fix this.

"If we had a dog," Ello stated through clenched teeth,

resurrecting their conversation from before, "then at least I'd have one friend in the world."

Instead of reflexively denying his daughter, Hunter considered it. A dog would love him, would greet him when he came home, would sit and stare beseechingly at meals instead of burying its attention in a phone. Maybe a member of the generation that *had it worse than any other generation in the history of the world* would cheer up a little, smile every once in a while, if they had a dog.

He glanced at his wife, and Juliana's expression was as unreadable as Sander's had been. She had to know he was actively contemplating it, because she could read him perfectly, but she wasn't sending back any signals. Was this some sort of test? If he agreed on a dog, would that be what broke up his marriage—the final injury, inflicted out of disregard? He was desperate to do whatever Juliana wanted, but how could he know what that *was*?

He pictured his wife feeding the dog, cleaning up its messes, giving it baths. Like a twin, but with the added ability to chew their footwear. That's exactly what would happen, even if the pet technically belonged to Ello.

*No,* he decided. Not until things were back to normal with his marriage.

"Well," he countered, "maybe you'll make friends with Sean O'Brien."

Ello recoiled in such disgust, it was as if the twins had just vomited on her. "Oh my God, Dad, you have no idea what it is like to be a teenager. Life sucks! This family sucks!"

Ello bolted from the room, nearly running over her grandfather as Sander made his way to the table.

"You shouldn't let her behave like that," Sander chided helpfully.

At school the next morning, Mourgen was standing in the front hallway as if she had been appointed as the welcoming committee.

Ello eyed her suspiciously. Long ago, Mourgen had gone all goth: black clothes, black lipstick, and a nose piercing she wasn't allowed to wear in school. Now, though, she was back to dressing like Brittne: short skirt, nice sweater, a bracelet, and her hair blond—well, orange, really, the intended color unable to fully transition from ebony in a single application of bleach. *Wait, is that Brittne's sweater?* Brittne only loaned apparel to her closest friends. In what twisted, parallel universe was Ello living now?

Mourgen even displayed the sweater like Brittne, her bony shoulders and thin torso showing off a waifish figure. She wore a sly expression, staring pointedly at Ello's chest. "Hey, so, Ello. I hear you got your glow up, but you been hiding it all this time."

"What? No," she replied shakily. "Of course not."

"Uh-huh."

Flustered, Ello turned and walked away from Mourgen, so disoriented that it took her a moment to notice that the usual girls were not in the usual places. The hallway seemed oddly out of sorts, as if people had taken up surreptitious positions. She saw the shadow of someone darting into a doorway, and someone else lurking behind an open locker door, horror-movie style. *Now what?*

She opened her locker and shrugged off her coat. She grabbed a notebook and was about to slam the metal door when she spotted a thick envelope she had not put there. Glancing around and noting the deliberate lack of people surveilling her, Ello pulled out the envelope, which was lumpy inside. She opened the flap and out spilled a handful of photographs.

She instantly recognized them, because they were photographs of *her*.

They were the wallet-sized school photos that everyone exchanged at the beginning of school each year. There were smiling pictures dating all the way back to first grade, photos Ello had given to her friends over the years.

Someone had used pins to poke out all of the eyes.

With fingers trembling from quakes deep inside her stomach, Ello flipped over the first one, a fifth-grade picture, on the back of which her own girlish scrawl declared, "We will always be friends, Mourgen. Love, E." There was one dedicated to Jayneigh, another from a different grade to Mourgen, and when she turned over the next one, she saw what she knew she would find: "To Brittne, my best friend forever. Love, E."

Ello realized she was holding her breath, but when she sucked in a fresh lungful of air, she still couldn't breathe. She stuffed the wretched pictures back in their envelope and tossed it into the depths of her locker. She grabbed her coat, forehanded the door, and nearly ran for the principal's office, narrowing her peripheral vision so as to catch no one's eye.

# CHAPTER EIGHT

What stuck with Juliana, what visited her at night like a ghost from the attic, was the expression on Hunter's face when she'd told him she wasn't happy in their marriage. She could see the words landing like body blows. Once they came out, there was no putting them back in, but now Juliana had different words.

A senior partner at Juliana's former law firm had a term for what she had done—he called it a "Gong Bong." It happened when something slipped out in court that the jury, regardless of the judge's instructions, could not ignore, could not unhear. Those words lingered in the air like the resonating *bong* from a gong struck with a soft hammer.

She'd planned to drop the Gong Bong—"unhappy in our marriage"—only if Hunter had reacted insensitively to her pain. But instead she had done it in response to his irritating, can-do optimism. There was nothing here for him to *fix*. She simply needed him to *understand*.

"You were wrong," Juliana lectured herself in the minivan after dropping the boys at preschool. "Your happiness is not Hunter's responsibility."

At home, she continued the conversation with herself.

"So, now, here you are, in the middle of the day, running a bath." Her list of chores was facedown on the kitchen counter to silence it. Juliana watched the water as it pounded into the tub, a bath bomb in her hand. She felt chilled and achy and a bit nauseated. In truth, it felt a little like being pregnant, which was impossible. "You can't be," she told herself. "I mean, sometimes birth control fails, but isn't that human error? You'd never make that mistake."

She took a breath, considering. It wasn't as if their schedules afforded a lot of time for *that*. . . .

"But there were a few nights, maybe five or six weeks ago . . . When did you have your last period?" Her expression became wistful. "You should call Mom," she whispered.

Her mother shared Juliana's habit of speaking out loud and at length to herself. Juliana remembered when she was about Ello's age and she heard her mother say, *"Estou grávida." I'm pregnant.* Talk about Gong Bongs. . . . The young Juliana had thought she'd love her baby brother—and she did, when he was a baby and she was a big sister. Then he became a toddler and she became a babysitter. She understood perfectly why Ello eyed the twins with such distrustful loathing.

Juliana glanced at her watch, calculating the difference between Eastern Standard Time and Brasilia Time. It was just past noon there. Her mother would be in the kitchen, talking to herself while waiting for her husband to come home for the midday meal.

As if anticipating being used, Juliana's cell phone rang, skating a little across the slick surface of the countertop. She snagged it and saw it was Ello.

"Mom," her daughter greeted, "can I come home?"

Ello's voice was strangely tremulous, her normal life force extinguished, and Juliana was instantly alarmed. "What's wrong?"

"I'm sick."

"Sick? Do you have a fever, a headache, are you sick to your stomach?"

"Mom, *please.*"

It went straight to her heart, that plaintive voice, her little girl asking for a mother's help. Juliana turned off the bath. "Okay, sweetie. I'll be right there."

Juliana walked down the hall to advise Sander she was leaving, but he was lying faceup on his bed, his arms across his chest, pale as a corpse in a casket. Winstead thumped his tail once but otherwise didn't react to her appearance, the pair of them a study in motionlessness. Juliana sighed and headed for her car.

Ello was waiting at the school doors and pushed them open the second Juliana turned into the circular driveway. Once Ello had climbed into the car, she reached out, and for the first time in a long, long time, pulled her mother into a tight embrace.

"What's wrong, honey?" Juliana whispered, kissing her daughter's hair.

Ello shook her head. Whatever horrors were served up by eighth grade today, Juliana wouldn't be hearing about them. Her daughter was choosing to face them alone.

Juliana struggled for something to say. Finally she managed, "I'm feeling a little ill myself."

*I'm praying I'm not pregnant,* she didn't add.

Today was it, D-Day, Liftoff, Game On, and Hunter had to go, had to get to work, but he couldn't, not without speaking to Juliana.

Garrett and Ewan were in the kitchen, attempting to yank a cabinet door open past the child lock that was frustrating their attempts to reach the toxic chemicals within.

Hunter frowned at them. "Where's your mom?"

Garrett said something that sounded sort of like "Pennsylvania." Hunter began searching the house. He'd been unaware of Juliana leaving bed; he only knew that, when he snapped open his eyes, she was not in her place next to him.

She wasn't doing laundry, she wasn't in the bathroom upstairs, and she wasn't in the garage. This was unusual enough that Hunter felt a tickle of concern. He tapped lightly on his daughter's door and pushed it open. "Ello, do you have any idea where Mom might be?"

Ello turned her back on him violently. "God, Dad. It's Thanksgiving. It's my *vacation*. I'm trying to sleep in."

Sighing, Hunter broadened the perimeters of his search. Finally, he descended into the finished part of the basement, where he heard a noise. The bathroom door was open a crack, and when he peeked in he could see his wife kneeling in front of the toilet bowl. "Oh my God, honey, are you okay?"

Juliana gave him a sad, depleted look. Then she retched, nothing coming up, but spat and flushed the toilet anyway.

"What are you doing down here?" he asked. Meaning, *Why here in the basement?*

"I didn't want to wake you up," she explained weakly, her voice echoing oddly out of the ceramic sound chamber of the bowl.

"Wake me up? How long have you been down here?"

"Since, I don't know, maybe four o'clock."

Hunter knelt next to his wife, feeling intense shame. Would *he* have been this considerate at four o'clock in the morning, padding silently down to this small bathroom where he could be sick without disturbing others?

"I'm sorry," he told her inadequately. "Do you want to go to the hospital?"

Juliana shook her head and gave him an anemic, but brave, grin. "So, today's the big day, right? You start the installation."

Hunter nodded. "Right. The workers are at the office right now, dismantling all the old furniture."

"You'd better go," she urged softly.

Hunter shook his head, suffused with tender affection. "Let's get you back up to bed."

Winstead followed Daddy down the hall to the kitchen. Hunter was already there, trying to pull Garrett out of his high chair.

Daddy regarded the scene with his arms crossed. "Where's my breakfast?" he demanded.

Winstead, sniffing at the floor, eased over to where the twins were seated. At mealtime, he could depend on them to rain a steady shower of crumbs his way.

"Dad," Hunter responded wearily, "Juliana's sick."

Winstead located a small piece of cheese and scarfed it up with gusto.

"I've got to get to the office. I'm late. I need your help," Hunter told his father.

Daddy grunted and Winstead eyed him, unsure what the sound meant.

Hunter angled his head toward the ceiling. "Ello? Ello, come down here!" he bellowed. He looked around. "My coffee cup's here somewhere."

"What do you expect me to do?" Daddy asked churlishly.

Though something odd seemed to be happening among the humans, Winstead couldn't comprehend what it might be. With a sigh, he collapsed to the floor, his nose placed squarely between the two high chairs in case of more falling morsels.

"These next three days are the most important in my career," Hunter informed his father. "Phase one has already commenced. By this time tomorrow, we'll be installing all-new furniture. It's a huge project, and I've got to be there to make sure it goes okay."

The house echoed with what sounded like a horse falling down the stairs. Winstead glanced at the doorway as Ello scuffed into the kitchen. "God, Dad," she groused.

"Listen to me," Hunter commanded, finally hoisting Garrett out of his high chair and placing him where Winstead could lick the food from his pants. Hunter reached for Ewan and began tugging him out as well. "Everyone listen to me. I have to go to the office. Okay? Your mom is sick, she's been throwing up half the night, and she's sleeping now. Keep checking on her, and, I don't know, just take care of everything."

Ello stared in disbelief. "It's Thanksgiving. What are we supposed to do about it?"

"I don't know, Ello," Hunter responded testily. "Maybe cook a turkey? Okay? Dad, can you help?"

There was a long, frozen silence as the question hung in the air.

"I hate this!" Ello cried. "Mom does everything and neither one of you ever help. It's so unfair."

Winstead cringed from the harsh voices, though it didn't stop him from sniffing Ewan's pants before the boys fled the kitchen.

"Yeah, of course," Daddy said in flat, uninvolved tones. "I can help Ello." He turned to her. "Can you fry me some eggs?"

Ello buried her face in her hands.

# CHAPTER NINE

S o," Sander speculated after his son had left. "How hard can it be to cook a turkey?"

He saw the tidal forces of rage fighting for control of Ello's face. As a little girl, she had been able to charm her grandfather into reading her one book after another after another. Now, though, she'd morphed into this hideously unpleasant creature, spitting acidic venom. He remembered being her age and helping his father in the woodshop. Ello and her whole generation expected everything to be handed to them.

"The turkey. The dressing. The pumpkin pie. The banana bread. The peas and carrots. The mashed potatoes and gravy. The salad," Ello cataloged scornfully. "How hard can it be?"

"I didn't say how hard would it be for *you* to cook a turkey, Ello. We'll do it together. We'll open some cans."

Ello groaned and Sander resisted the urge to throw up his hands and walk out on her. "Okay," he proclaimed with false enthusiasm, looking around the kitchen as if seeing it for the first time, "let's consult a cookbook."

"Grandpa," Ello chided, "nobody uses a cookbook anymore. You just look it up online."

"I don't trust the Internet," Sander replied loftily. "It's nothing but lies."

"That's just stupid."

"Watch your tone, young lady."

A violent noise came from the back of the house. It sounded as if the twins had managed to tip over their bunk beds. Sander winced, and even Winstead reacted, staring in alarm toward where the percussion still echoed through the house.

Ello mockingly raised her eyebrows at her grandfather. "How hard can it be?"

*Enough.* "I've just about had it with your attitude," he snapped. "You saying you can't be bothered to help your parents with Thanksgiving? Fine. Go stare at your phone."

Her eyes widened. "*My* attitude? What about you? You just sit in your chair all day. You don't help with anything. You *stink*." Ello pinched her nose with her fingers. "I bring you your stupid fried eggs every morning and *you've never thanked me*. When you moved in, Mom said it was temporary, but you just stay and stay and stay! That was supposed to be my bedroom, I would have my own bathroom, except you *live* there." Winstead, sensing trouble, clicked across the hard floor to nose Sander's hand.

"Do you think I wanted to move here?" he shot back. "I spent all my money on experimental procedures my insurance wouldn't cover. And then my wife died anyway."

"Yes! Grandma died! But that's not my fault!" she shouted.

He regarded her silently, the anger seeping out of him. At that moment, if he could have willed himself a fatal heart attack, he would have done so. He wanted to just crumple to the floor. "No," he admitted after a long moment. "You're right. It's not your fault."

Hot tears were flowing down Ello's cheeks. "I do chores. I do the laundry. *Your* laundry. And school is really hard, and I hate my life. The twins are all anybody cares about."

"That's not true."

"Nobody knows what I'm going through! You all just act like I should be happy. But I'm *not* happy!" she screamed. Her face had turned red, her chest heaving from the effort of carrying so much anger.

"I'm not particularly happy at this juncture, either," Sander observed wryly. "Thank you for bringing my fried eggs every morning, Ello."

His granddaughter went to the counter and pulled out a tissue, blowing her nose.

"You think I'm a worthless old man," Sander murmured.

She didn't look at him.

"And you know what? Maybe you're right. No, not maybe. I *am* worthless. I have no function whatsoever. If I don't get out of bed in the morning, it matters to nobody."

Winstead sat, watching Sander alertly, and made an almost inaudible whine.

"You're right, Ello. I'm wrong. And I'm sorry. And I do care about you. Before she died, all Barbara wanted to do was have you come visit. And you brought such joy, we never wanted to give you back to your parents."

"Well, I wish you hadn't," Ello declared forcefully.

"It took some sand to speak to me like that just now."

"Sand?" Ello looked puzzled.

"Courage. I'm a lot bigger than you are."

"Yeah, well, I could still take you." A shadow of a grin touched her lips.

Sander mentally hugged his granddaughter. He figured that was all she'd allow . . . an imaginary embrace. He cleared his throat. "Well, I'm about to make the worst Thanksgiving dinner in history. Wanna join me?"

Hunter watched morosely as his crew members worked on dismantling the aging cubicle furniture on the engineering floor. By his calculation, they were falling three minutes behind for every one minute they worked. Though they were earning double time, none of the workers seemed to believe that that meant they should do anything but work at a pace appropriate for a holiday. More than once, he'd been forced to chase them out of the break room, where they were sitting, drinking soda from the refrigerator, and relating tales of furniture-assembly past. A year from now, they would probably tell each other, "Remember that time when we were paid all that money and didn't do any work?"

His cell phone rang—it was his daughter.

"Hey, Dad," Ello greeted him breezily. "How's it going?"

Hunter had decided many years ago not to burden his children with work issues. "Okay," he lied.

"So, Ewan sort of flushed Garrett's pillow down the toilet."

"Sort of?"

"Grandpa can see it, but he can't get it out. He wants to cut it up and pull it out in chunks, but we're afraid of Garrett's reaction. It's his favorite pillow, the one he calls 'Cuh-ha.' I think it means cupcake."

"Maybe turn off the water, remove the toilet, and pull it out from below?" Hunter suggested.

"Like Grandpa could do something like that. You should see the gravy he made. It has all these lumps in it."

"Your grandfather used to build houses, honey."

"Not anymore."

"Sweetie," Hunter nearly pleaded, "I really have to go."

"We had the most major fight, like, ever in history."

Hunter gripped the phone. "Oh?" he replied warily.

"Yeah. He said he's sorry about how everyone treats me like I'm the maid."

"I'm sure that's exactly what he said."

"Anyway," Ello continued lightly, "the turkey's going to be ready pretty early, like, by maybe three o'clock? It looks done now, actually."

"Oh, honey," Hunter replied.

"Come on, Dad, it's Thanksgiving. You have to come home."

Hunter sighed. Maybe the workers would do a better job if he were not hovering over them in obvious panic. "How's Mom?"

"I went in to check on her a few minutes ago. She was sound asleep. I think she's okay. I don't think she's going to want dinner, though. Which might be true of all of us. The turkey's . . . well, the skin is really, really brown, but the meat is still running red juices. So it will be crispy on the outside and fatal on the inside."

Hunter laughed.

"You know, Dad, if anything ever happens to Mom, you and Grandpa should probably just join the Navy or something. Someplace where they have to cook for you. I could move to California and we could put the twins in an orphanage."

Hunter laughed again, then realized he'd been missing something—Ello was in an upbeat mood. How in the world had *that* happened?

"Nothing's going to happen to your mom," Hunter assured her. Because, of course, he assumed it was true.

Amazingly, Ello and Sander had actually managed to pull things together pretty well. It was true that the oleaginous gravy was goopy and full of little pockets of white powder. The dressing was soup; the turkey, sawed into uneven shingles on the oval platter, was overcooked; the pumpkin pie hot and wet. The twins had placed toy cars around the turkey centerpiece. Despite it all, Sander and Ello were smiling proudly at each other when they served Hunter his plate.

Ewan picked up a pea, lifting it toward his nostril with obvious intent.

"Ewan!" Hunter commanded sharply. "Do not put peas up your nose."

Ewan stared in astonishment. "Ewa?"

Hunter turned to Ello.

"You said not to put peas up his nose, and he said, 'Ever?'" Ello translated.

Garrett's eyes were bright with the possibilities afforded him by all the artillery on his plate: peas, carrots, turkey. Winstead wagged encouragement from below.

"No!" Hunter warned sternly. "Behave."

For the moment, both boys seemed startled into compliance.

"We did pretty well, if I do say so myself," Sander remarked. He and Ello exchanged proud grins.

Hunter blinked. What in the world had happened to forge an alliance between those two?

Over turkey, he contemplated the family ritual of asking every person to say what they were thankful for this Thanksgiving holiday. Then he decided against it. What would Ello say? *I'm thankful hormones have hijacked my personality?* And what about Sander? *I'm glad I'm still drawing breath?* Even though Hunter was pretty sure Dad felt exactly the opposite. And Hunter himself—*I'm thankful my whole career is going to sink or swim based on a few million dollars' worth of furniture?*

When his phone rang, Ello dashed into the living room to fetch it without being asked. Hunter had meant to bring it to the table with him. He blanched when he saw the caller: Mrs. O'Brien.

"I'm surprised you are not here supervising," Mrs. O'Brien said by way of holiday greeting. "Nothing seems to be getting accomplished, despite the fact that we're paying these workers double time, something I will remind you was *your* idea."

"Yes, but it's still cheaper per hour than paying engineers to stand around if they can't work starting Monday morning. This really is the most cost-effective way," he assured her. The mathematical case for this had been laid out in the moving plan, but he didn't remind her.

"I assume you'll be returning shortly?" Mrs. O'Brien asked in a not-a-question tone.

"Of course—I was just having a quick Thanksgiving dinner with my family." The words hung in the air, heavy with implications. *Thanksgiving. Family.*

"Good," Mrs. O'Brien said dismissively.

"Happy Thanksgiving," Hunter couldn't stop himself from saying.

Mrs. O'Brien hung up without replying.

Juliana opened her eyes when she sensed Hunter leaning over her.

"How do you feel?" he asked.

She shook her head. *Depleted, mostly.*

Hunter pressed a palm against her forehead. She knew it was not hot.

"Do you want to go to the emergency room? Should I at least call the doctor?" he asked anxiously.

Juliana licked her lips. "No," she whispered in a weak voice. "I'll be fine."

"Okay. . . ."

"Hunter?"

"Yes?"

"What would happen if I'm . . ." Pregnant. *Grávida*.

"If you're . . . ?"

She shook her head. "Never mind."

# CHAPTER TEN

Juliana felt better on Saturday—well enough, she told Hunter, to take Ello to ice dancing.

For Hunter, it was the most critical day in the entire installation process. The furniture was almost all moved out—only the executive offices remained.

The work crew reported to a man named Monty. Hunter had met a dog named Monty once, but this was his first human.

Monty sported a thick mustache and a bald head. He liked to call Hunter "Bossman." Hunter had been called worse.

"Okay, Bossman," Monty said, "we're unloading the new work spaces onto the engineering floor for assembly now. And the other crew's getting started on the executive offices."

"We're behind schedule," Hunter fretted, not for the first time.

Monty shrugged. "That's not our fault. Things are taking longer than we expected."

Hunter nodded as if this made any sense. If it wasn't their fault, whose was it?

Then a loud *boom* echoed through the building. Hunter looked at Monty, who wore a puzzled expression.

"What was that?" Hunter asked.

Monty shook his head. He reached out to stroke his thick mustache, as if checking to make sure the thing was still there. "Don't know, Bossman."

They were walking down the hall toward the noise when they heard another, similar *boom,* this time from an office much closer. Alarmed, Hunter picked up his pace. He looked in an open doorway and saw a pair of movers standing and regarding an executive desk with disgusted expressions. The hutch had completely collapsed, scissoring flat.

"What happened?" Hunter demanded.

One of the men shrugged. "Thing just fell apart," he observed in distaste.

*Boom.* Another hutch down.

Hunter turned and dashed across the hall into an office where two more movers were pulling a desk and hutch away from the wall. He watched helplessly as the shelves pancaked with a crash.

"Wow," one of the movers admired.

From down the hallway: *Boom. Boom.*

"Stop!" Hunter yelled. He stepped out of the office. "Everyone stop moving the desks!" he shouted as loudly as he could.

*Boom.*

❄

Monty produced a pack of gum from his pocket and extended it to Hunter the way smokers offer each other cigarettes. When Hunter shook his head, Monty pulled out a piece for himself and begin unwrapping it, taking much more care than the men moving Hunter's furniture. "It's not our fault," Monty observed. "Somebody removed the back panels from all the hutches. That gave them no lateral strength, so the second we moved 'em, the bookshelves just collapsed on themselves. Only reason they stayed up was because they were supported by the wall." Monty nodded, satisfied with his testimony. "Bam," he concluded.

"Sounds like the sort of thing that maybe your crew could have looked into before trying to move the executive furniture," Hunter suggested.

Monty stuck the wad of gum in his mouth and examined the foil wrapping as if it were a fortune from a cookie. "Yeah, maybe, Bossman."

By the time Hunter's cries of "stop" suggested to the moving teams that perhaps they should, well, stop, only two desks had upright, intact hutches on them.

"Can they be repaired?" Hunter pressed anxiously.

Monty shrugged. "Thing is, the shelves were all just cheap pressboard with veneer. When they collapsed, the screws ripped out and took a pretty big chunk of shelving with them. What we would call holes."

"What would a layman call them?"

"Sorry?"

"Look, I *sold* that furniture to the CFO of a start-up

that just got a little funding. I don't know if he'll want any of the units, now," Hunter explained a bit desperately.

Monty nodded. "Most start-ups fail," he noted.

"Which is relevant because . . . ?"

Monty opened his mouth to air out his gum. "Huh?"

That was how Hunter's morning began. He directed Monty to have his crew take the desks to the loading dock, sans hutches, calculating that maybe by Monday someone would come up with a way out of the mess. The day drained into night. By 6 P.M. the following day, Sunday, the installation was scheduled to be complete. It wasn't. They still had at least ten hours to go.

Hunter had not left the building, drawing all of his nutrition from coffee.

"Gonna suck if people start coming to work tomorrow and we're not done, Bossman," Monty informed him helpfully through his gum.

"If that happens, then we begin losing serious money while we have highly paid software engineers standing around, unable to work. Not your fault," Hunter finished, simply to spare himself from hearing it come out of Monty's lips.

Monty agreed, blowing a bubble.

"You are not pregnant," Juliana told herself with relief Monday morning. She flushed the toilet and staggered back to bed, feeling dizzy. "You're just sick. You have the flu." She frowned. Her pulse was fluttery, her head light, her stomach sore and weak. "But at least you're not pregnant. *Não grávida.*"

Later, when Juliana entered the kitchen, feeling shaky and weak, her husband was sitting at the table staring at a piece of toast on a plate as if watching for signs of life.

"What time did you get home?" she asked him, going automatically to the coffee maker.

"A little while ago."

"Do you want your coffee? You left it here next to the pot."

"That would be great, thanks."

Juliana heated the cup in the microwave before taking it to him. "Did you get the project finished the way you wanted?"

Hunter raised his wrist and stared at his watch as if he had never seen it before. Finally, he shrugged. "Supposed to be done. When I left, they said another half hour. So, figure an hour. Right about now, employees are probably arriving and the moving crew's pulling away from the back entrance like it was a bank robbery."

"Honey," Juliana said, "you look like I felt all weekend. You should get some sleep."

He nodded. "Soon as I get the kids off to school."

Hunter's words warmed Juliana from within. She went to him and put a tender hand on his shoulder. "I'm okay to drive," she told him. "Seriously, you need to rest."

Hunter stood, yawning. "Thank you," he said. "Oh, and don't forget to pick up Sean O'Brien. I wrote down his address on a sticky and put it on the refrigerator." They both turned and looked. Hunter frowned. "Well, I put it *somewhere*," he corrected himself.

"I think Ello's pretty unhappy with the idea of guiding the boy through his first day at school," Juliana observed tactfully. *Actually, she's freaking out and has already thrown a tantrum about it.*

Hunter grunted. "Well, it can't be helped. I really, really need points with my boss right now."

Ello watched the curbside piles of dirty snow glide past the minivan's passenger-side window, not speaking to her mother. This was going to be the Worst Day Of Her Life. She pictured this Sean O'Brien, some farmer from Detroit, following her around like an imprinted goose. Where was she supposed to sit at lunch? She couldn't guide him to her usual table. That would get her Banned For Life.

Brittne ate during the other lunch period, so at least Ello was spared *that*. She groaned, not for the first time that morning, pulled out her phone, and stared at it. Brittne had not responded to any of her texts. Send another one?

"The thing with the school photos was just a joke," Ello stated aloud. That's how she was playing it. Something so insignificant, it wasn't like Everyone Was Staring, whispering, laughing.

*Please,* Ello thought to herself, almost a prayer. *Please, Brittne.*

The Michigan sky matched her mood perfectly: gray, oppressive, dull.

"This is it," her mom announced, pulling into the driveway of a new and pricey two-story home. "Nice place."

Ello flicked a glance at the house, then looked away without comment. She was pretty sure she was going to throw up. They sat for a moment, the twins oddly quiet, probably reacting to the unexpected change in their morning routine.

"Maybe he's sick and can't go to school today," Ello suggested hopefully.

As soon as she said this, the door opened and a boy bounded out, smiling.

Ello glanced at him, then stared at him. *This* was Sean O'Brien? He was as tall as any boy in her class. He looked athletic and muscular, and his blond hair was thick and combed to the side. As he approached, she saw that his eyes were a piercing blue.

He was almost breathtakingly handsome.

Sean O'Brien sauntered around to Juliana's window, which she lowered.

"Mrs. Goss?" he greeted jovially.

Juliana was smiling. Ello assumed most people couldn't help but smile at this boy—he radiated happiness, as if he'd never known a moment of bad mood in his life.

"Hi, Sean." Juliana turned. "Ello, why don't you get in back with the twins and let Sean ride up with me."

Ello, too stunned to speak, wordlessly slid out of the car. Sean came around the front, grinning at her. "So, you're Eloise?" he guessed. "You're going to give me the grand tour today? I really appreciate it."

It occurred to Ello that she should say something. "Yes," she grated hoarsely.

"Her friends call her Ello," Juliana told Sean.

"Ello!" Sean confirmed with delight.

Ello slid in next to Ewan, brushing away the chunks of donut he had tossed on the seat. The twins peered at her as if they had never seen her before. Sean buckled in, and as Juliana was backing down the driveway, turned and tossed another dazzling smile at Ello. "I'm really looking forward to this," he told her. Though that seemed impossible to Ello—they were headed to *middle school*—Sean obviously meant it.

So, okay, maybe he wasn't too bright. Somehow, Ello had the sense she could overlook that.

At 11 A.M., Hunter struggled to drag his state of being into wakefulness. He applied jumper cables to his nervous system with two hasty cups of coffee, but he'd clearly built up too much immunity over the past several days. The car drove itself to his office, Hunter blinking away what felt like sand in the gears of his eyelids.

The receptionist, Kim, glared at him with her pale brown eyes as he walked in the front door. "Well, *you* look like crap," she observed. She tossed her head, her tight, sandy curls rippling with the motion.

"Yeah," Hunter agreed.

Kim theoretically reported to Hunter, as did all the general office staff. Kim did not seem to believe this.

"So, how's it going with the installation? Everybody like their new setup?" he asked.

Kim's expression seemed a little odd to Hunter, as if she had taken a bite of something and was trying to figure out what it was. "I guess you could say that, maybe, a little."

Hunter shrugged. "It might take them a while to get used to it. But all the studies show that a more open floor plan results in more collaboration, especially where it's most needed, in the engineering department."

"You look that up on Wikipedia?" Kim challenged him scornfully.

Hunter simply shook his head. Kim reached into her drawer and pulled out Hunter's moving plan, all two hundred pages of it, in a ring binder. She dropped it on her desk with a *thump*. "So, can I throw this away now?"

"No, not yet. There are still tasks to be completed."

"I never even read the thing," Kim advised contemptuously.

"I guess I'll go up to engineering and see how it's going," he responded.

Kim shrugged her apathy.

Hunter rode the elevator up to what he was counting on to earn him his promotion—the engineering floor, where everyone pulled in six-figure salaries. Added productivity in software development would instantly show up on the company's bottom line.

When the doors eased open and Hunter stepped off the elevator, he gasped.

The new collaborative pods were all in place. The cubicle walls were gone. The software engineers should have been *"buzzing like bees in a hive, cross-pollinating their ideas"* (a direct quote from the manufacturer's sales brochure). Instead, they had apparently gone to the loading dock and grabbed the large cardboard boxes in which the furniture was shipped. Using packing tape, they had erected tall barriers between themselves and their compatriots, completely cocooning themselves in brown walls with FRAGILE—THIS SIDE UP printed on them.

Some of the THIS SIDE UP notices were upside down.

Okay. Obviously, this was a joke. Whereas the developers were supposed to be facing each other over a low divider, they had instead walled themselves off on three sides. *Ha ha*, they'd be saying, *wait until Hunter sees this! We will all get a good chuckle from his reaction for sure, ha ha. This is the kind of hilarious hijinks we software guys come up with, ha ha.*

Hunter forced a jaunty grin onto his features. He could take a joke; he had a sense of humor. "Hey, Stephen," he said, greeting one of the software engineers. "So, pretty funny, these walls."

Stephen often rode his bike to work and had prescription goggles so he wouldn't crash into Michigan potholes. For some reason, he had given up wearing regular glasses no matter what his transportation, and he was goggled now, peering owlishly through thick, rubber-lined, protruding lenses, as if he'd come to the office in an open cockpit.

"What?"

"I mean, the cardboard," Hunter explained, his grin cracking from the effort of holding it in place.

"Huh?"

Hunter dropped all pretense. "What's with the boxes?"

Stephen blinked at him with magnified eyeballs. "Someone took down the cubicles."

This non-answer made Hunter want to slap the goggles off the man's face. "Yes," he agreed between clenched teeth, "that's by design. This way, people on a project can collaborate and even overhear conversations that will make them more effective."

"Collaborate." Stephen shook his head. "See, that's not how I work. I don't *want* to collaborate. I don't like people. That's why I'm a software engineer."

"Well, sure, that's the thing. . . . The layout's conducive to working together, even if some people don't like it."

"I liked the way things were. Everybody did, okay? If you make me take down the cardboard, I'll quit."

Hunter nodded numbly. Since being hired, he'd assumed that everyone saw the same problems he did: people surrounded by other individuals, yet not ever interacting, spending all their time in solitary confinement. Emails as inflammatory as Twitter posts because the sender had no personal relationship with the recipient. Low morale. Isolation.

Now he understood that what he saw as a debilitating flaw was, for some, a coveted way of life.

So what had been designed to be a gorgeous new office,

populated with cheerful, interactive engineers, instead had grown into an ugly maze of refrigerator boxes.

Hunter tried to breathe. It was difficult to imagine a worse failure.

He felt a tap on his arm and turned. Kim handed him his cell phone. "You left this on my desk," she admonished, in the same tone she would have used had he decorated her blotter with a dead rodent.

"Thanks."

"Also, Mrs. O'Brien wants to see you in her office," she advised neutrally.

"Okay. I'll be there in a minute."

"I think now. Like, the way she said it."

Hunter was aware of Stephen monitoring this exchange. "Thanks, Kim."

"So, you need to go see her," Kim added firmly.

Hunter sighed. What he did not say was that he didn't *want* to talk to Mrs. O'Brien.

# CHAPTER ELEVEN

Ello didn't know if people were staring at her because she was with Sean O'Brien, or because Brittne had used her witchery on the student body to transform Ello into a dead girl walking. Either way, she felt as if a thousand pairs of eyes were watching her every move.

Ello escorted Sean to the office, where they confirmed that he was enrolled but had not yet been assigned any classes. The vice principal suggested that Ello take Sean with her on her own schedule while the staff tried to figure out who was to blame for what had not happened.

Sean seemed implausibly jubilant at the idea of spending the day on Ello's elbow.

"So, you moved from Detroit?" Ello asked him as they moved through the crowded hallway. She Would Not Look At Anyone But Him.

Her question made him smile. Everything made him smile. And his smile was one of the cutest things about him. It made her want to grin back, like they had some shared joke.

*He even has dimples.*

"Yeah," he affirmed. "We lived there for three years.

Before that, Vancouver. Have you ever been to Vancouver? It's in Canada. But it's not, like, freezing cold, the way it is, well, here. It's at sea level, but there are mountains. Do you ski?"

Ello did not ski, had not been to Vancouver, and was, compared to Sean O'Brien, a Complete Loser. If he cared about any of that, he didn't comment.

On their way to third-period history with Mr. Morrison, Ello felt Brittne's icy stare tracking her as she strolled next to Sean. Ello did not return the look. It felt surreal not to care more about Brittne than anything else in the world.

"Hey, do you ice-skate?" Sean asked abruptly.

Ello narrowed her eyes suspiciously. "Did my dad tell you to ask me that?"

Sean shook his head. The question (of course) made him smile. "No, it's just that I really love to skate. I've been playing hockey since I was like six years old. And my aunt teaches ice dancing."

"Ice dancing," Ello repeated.

"Yeah," Sean replied. "Do you know what that is? It's not figure skating, it's a different thing."

"I'm aware," Ello replied faintly.

Valerie O'Brien viewed Hunter with cold, hawklike eyes. "When were you going to tell me that you broke all of the executive furniture?"

Hunter's fuzzy brain processed the question a little slowly. "Now?" he guessed.

She pressed her lips into a bitter line. "What," she finally replied, "am I supposed to tell the CFO of that start-up when he calls to inform me all of the furniture we delivered to him is busted up?"

Hunter had a good answer for that one. He wondered what it was.

"Well, just see if you can talk them into not making us pay to have the junk removed, at least."

"Colfaxette Engineering," he finally replied. That was the name of the start-up, and Mrs. O'Brien, as far as he knew, had never spoken to anyone there.

She waved him off. "Whatever. Say we won't try to collect on our invoice, but if he wants *us* to pay *him,* he'll have to sue us. At this point, that's pretty much your only value to me. Have you been up to the engineering floor?"

Hunter nodded wearily.

"Well, it doesn't look very good, now does it, Hunter?" Mrs. O'Brien asked in a voice normally reserved for addressing delinquent children. "Everyone has boxes on their desks. You can barely walk around the room. They aren't collaborating; they're up there hiding like voles."

Hunter blinked. Voles?

"I didn't hire you, but I believe in giving people a chance to correct their screwups. So here's what I am going to do," Mrs. O'Brien continued. "I'll give you until we come back to work from the holidays in January. That gives you all of December to figure out what you're going to do about this mess you've created. If you haven't addressed the situation by then, I will not be requiring your so-called expertise any longer."

Hunter stared.

"I'm saying fix it or you're terminated," she translated for him.

Hunter nodded until he realized he'd been dismissed. He dazedly made his way to the men's room and concentrated on not letting his meager breakfast punch its way back out.

Hunter had never been fired before. Now it felt as if everything that defined him was leaking away.

He eventually lost the battle with breakfast.

Ello lived every day that week as if recording it in a diary. The school ultimately decided it was too late in the semester to care about Sean's schedule, so he just hung with Ello, her bodyguard against eighth-grade society.

*Dear Diary: I ate with Sean at lunch, we walked together to class, his locker is only three down from mine, Sean is so funny, Sean is so nice.*

*Dear Diary: Sean, Sean, Sean.*

She took the envelope of photographs with the pin-pricked eyes and, In Full View Of Everyone, dumped it in the trash in the hallway.

"What's that?" Sean asked innocently.

"A list of all my mistakes."

Sean laughed and everybody heard it, and the two of them walked to math as if Ello Didn't Care about how her supposed friends were treating her.

She was immune. Sean was her flu shot.

Had to be peer pressure, Hunter concluded. The employees who'd built medieval castles out of corrugated boxes were doing so only because everyone else was doing it. It was the software-engineer equivalent of a street riot. But how to prove something like that? A *survey,* he decided. A survey would flush out how they really felt about their new digs—which were, after all, top-of-the-line, high-tech expressions of the art of office furniture.

When the opinion cards came back, Hunter quickly established that, unsurprisingly, all of the executives were extremely happy with their new, nicer furniture. So, pretty much, were office workers like Kim. As for Kim, she always used pink ink, so he knew which card was hers. In response to the question, "On a scale of one to five, with one being extremely dissatisfied and five being very satisfied, how do you like your new furniture?" Kim had given him a four. Hunter had trouble picturing her ever being "very satisfied" with anything.

The engineers ignored the one-to-five scale and defiantly wrote out their answers, which yielded an outsized number of zeroes and negative integers. On average, rating the new digs from one to five, they gave it a zero point three.

Hunter stacked the cards, twisted a rubber band around them, and dropped them into an empty drawer with a defeated-sounding *thunk*.

Time to deal with the rest of this awful equation: Colfaxette Engineering, Inc., the company that had purchased the executive furniture with the collapsing hutches. Hunter dialed the number listlessly.

"Hi, Robert," Hunter greeted the voicemail. "It's Hunter Goss. I like to work through things on the phone rather than email, so would you give me a call at your convenience?"

Hunter did believe that unpleasant topics were best handled voice-to-voice, but he also believed people were more productive when they collaborated. He believed his daughter was still his little girl and that his wife still loved him. He was, he realized bitterly, completely wrong about everything in his whole miserable life.

Hunter slid into his seat at the table just as his family was digging into dinner. Sander had reheated some of Juliana's lasagna because she wasn't feeling up to dinner, either the making or the eating.

Hunter watched his family interact as if sitting behind one-way glass at a police station.

What would happen to these people when he lost his job? Would Juliana stick with an unemployed husband?

*Not happy in my marriage.*

*Oh, really? Well, you ain't seen nothin' yet. Wait until we can't afford food.*

After the lasagna, Hunter went back to check on his wife. Juliana was sleeping. He tenderly put a palm on each side of her face. She did not seem feverish—seemed, in fact, at utter peace.

Was he really losing her?

Thanksgiving had been only a week ago, and look how much had happened since then!

Sean O'Brien had happened.

Ello smiled, remembering how he had demonstrated in the hallway how he could skate backward, which of course was a total fail.

Sean loved hockey, so Ello pretended to like it too. She didn't tell him about her ice dancing, which was about as far from hockey as water polo. No one else in middle school was doing it. She pictured his scorn—*You mean, you skate around in circles and don't hit anybody?*

Ello turned to the mirror and her frown deepened as she took in her reflection. She hadn't given her outfit much thought, and had automatically donned a variation of her standard school uniform: a baggy sweatshirt. Yesterday it had been a baggy sweater. All because she still worried about Brittne, which was ridiculous. Not like Ello Could Help It.

Thinking of Brittne led to a check of her phone and there was, of course, no text. She turned away. "I guess the secret's out," she told herself. She pulled something from her closet she had never worn: a much tighter, much more revealing sweater made of thin, clingy cashmere. A perfect shade of green for her eyes. Brittne had never even seen it.

She turned left and right in front of her mirror. This would be okay. It wasn't like she was trying to be one of the Kardashians. There were many girls in her grade who were far more busty than Eloise Goss. Right? Come on.

Brushing her hair, she froze for a moment, remembering a packet of pictures with poked-out eyes. *You don't have any friends*, a cruel voice hissed from within.

*Sean O'Brien*, a different voice replied.

*Nobody texted you today.*

*Except Sean O'Brien.*

Ello exhaled. She painted on a small amount of lip gloss and a moisturizer with some pigment in it—pretty much all the makeup her dad would tolerate. She'd run a pencil through her brows when she made it to school. Then she'd add eyelid primer to even things out. Then she'd use a brush to apply a darker shade from a paint pot. Then a dark powder eyeshadow, and finally her Favorite Eyeliner In The World, plus a thick coat of mascara and fake eyelashes to Add Volume, then foundation, and then concealer, and then pigmented highlighter and a vivid lip gloss in a color her father had nicknamed Absolutely Not.

Thinking of her father, she froze again.

He had never seen this sweater either.

Hunter eased out of bed and padded into the kitchen to get breakfast going for his family for the second morning in a row, letting Juliana sleep. She had struggled throughout the night with her illness, twisting and bending as if sleeping with a Labrador.

Ello sauntered in as Hunter was frowning at the fried eggs he'd prepared for his father. Sander liked them basted. Yesterday, the eggs had stuck to the bottom of the pan and he'd broken the yolks with the spatula prying them out. Today, the eggs slid around like drunken eyeballs when he tipped the pan, leaving no room for his spoon to scoop up the butter to baste them.

It was discouraging to realize that the two things that could go wrong with fried eggs were that they would either stick to the bottom of the pan or they wouldn't.

He turned to ask his daughter if she had any tips and literally gasped. "What are you wearing?"

Ello glared back in stony defiance.

"Ello? You cannot wear that to school."

Ello sneered at him. "Mom bought it for me *for school*."

"You'll die of exposure." Hunter glanced at his twin sons, as if seeking male moral support. They were both kicking in their high chairs like synchronized swimmers doing the backstroke. He turned back to his daughter, gesturing with his spatula. "When did this . . ." He simply lacked words for what he was trying to ask.

"God. . . ." Ello groaned. "Why can't you for once be normal?" She snatched the tray containing Sander's breakfast and turned away.

As she stormed out, Hunter reflected on the question. Had he *ever* been normal?

The boys quit kicking and fixated on pinching Cheerios between their fingers and stuffing them into their mouths, so he elected to leave them for the moment.

Juliana was sitting up in bed, looking wan.

"I need to talk to you," he said tersely, then hesitated. "You okay? You didn't sleep much last night."

Juliana nodded wearily. "Finally feeling better. What's wrong, honey?"

"We have an urgent situation. A family emergency."

She raised her eyebrows for him to go on.

"Your daughter has developed these . . . these . . ." Hunter cupped his hands over his pectorals. "It's like she's become a . . . God, I don't know, a . . . a . . ."

"Mammal?" Juliana suggested.

"Stop smiling. This is serious. It's a serious situation. I mean it. Stop laughing! We have to do something."

"Like what?"

"I don't think I'm explaining myself very well. Remember how she looked just yesterday? Well now she's got these protuberances. She's protuberating!"

"Hunter," Juliana soothed, "your daughter is a teenager. That means things are going to be changing."

"No," Hunter decided.

Juliana laughed.

"Not like *this*. Not this quickly. Changes like this are supposed to be slow, like over a decade. Give us time to deal with it. To, I don't know. Find ways to disguise it."

"Do you honestly mean to tell me this is the first time you've noticed how your daughter is maturing?"

"Of course. Fathers don't look at that."

Juliana laughed again, then spasmed as it turned into a cough.

Hunter regarded his wife with concern. "Should we think about taking you to the emergency room?"

"No, no," Juliana assured him. "I'm sure I'll feel better today. Can you stay home from work this morning and take the twins to preschool?"

Hunter attempted to prevent his answer from showing up on his face, but she knew him too well. Her shoulders slumped.

"Don't worry. Dad will do it," he assured her.

"Sander?" she replied skeptically.

"I just really need to be at work right now," he told her, wringing the desperation from his words.

A few minutes later, Hunter was standing in his father's doorway. "Hey, Dad," he said by way of greeting. "So if it's still okay, I'd like you to drive everyone this morning again."

"My eggs were not basted," Sander replied.

Hunter nodded. "Sure," he agreed.

"I like them basted."

"This is known to be true."

Sander regarded him with a where-did-I-go-wrong-as-a-father expression.

Hunter sighed in exasperation. "I'm leaving now. Okay? Dad? You got this?"

His father's expression remained sour. Apparently the titanic tragedy of breakfast was something the family would have trouble getting past.

"I suppose," Sander said at last.

"Just make sure Ello puts on a coat. Like, she has this big parka. All puffy?"

On Friday, Hunter despondently left another voicemail for the CFO of Colfaxette, sticking to his story that they needed to have an actual conversation, but leaving out the part about Hunter having sold the man a bunch of broken furniture. Aside from that, he accomplished almost nothing as he regarded the shantytown-like display of cardboard boxes that warrened off the engineers and their co-conspirators. He had once enjoyed this, walking around like a prince strolling the royal grounds, surveying his domain. Now, though, he felt as if the peasants were coming after him with torches and pitchforks.

It was late afternoon when Kim found him in the break room, idly assessing the extent to which Kim had over-purchased herbal tea. Only she liked the stuff. The programmers lived on caffeine and sugar.

"Your daughter's on the landline," Kim advised curtly.

Hunter patted his pockets. "I'm not sure where I left my cell phone," he confessed.

"I have better things to do than answering your phone calls," she warned him.

Hunter frowned, because answering calls was what Kim was paid to *do*. As Hunter moved to leave, she reminded him, "Don't forget your coffee cup." He grabbed it and went to his office.

There was something about the way Ello said "Dad?" that stabbed him. He gripped the phone. "What's wrong?" he asked.

"Can you come home?"

He stayed his reflexive response. Of course he couldn't go home right now—he was at work. Instead, he repeated his question. "What's wrong?"

"It's Mom. She's really sick."

# CHAPTER TWELVE

The emergency-room physician was tall and dark-skinned and reassuring. Hunter grasped the words he offered like life preservers tossed down to him after he'd fallen over the ship's rails.

*Not unusual. I am not too concerned. Dehydrated. Antibiotics.*

Still, Hunter's hands trembled as he signed the necessary papers. Juliana gave him a feeble smile when they wheeled her down the wide hallway. He unconsciously brought his knuckles to his teeth as they hooked her up to an IV. He held her hand the rest of the afternoon and didn't even notice when the sun eased below the horizon.

His daughter and his father were waiting for him when he arrived home around midnight, leaping to their feet as soon as he walked in the door. "Ello," he observed without any heat, "you should really be in bed."

Ello swatted the words away. "How's Mom? How could you not reply to my texts? Did you lose your cell phone again? On a day like *today*?"

Hunter fixed her with a steady gaze. "They said she's comfortable and stable. They think it's a UTI—urinary tract infection. They're giving her an IV of antibiotics. It's a common thing. I'm pretty sure she's going to be fine. They told me I should come home and get some rest. Okay? They said nothing to worry about. Tomorrow's Saturday. Everyone should just go on doing what they would normally be doing."

Sander's face was unreadable, and Hunter flashed back to a similar conversation from when Barbara had first been diagnosed. Needing to push that thought out of his head, he changed the subject. "Dad, can you take Ello to ice dancing in the morning?"

Ello's gaze slid away evasively as he asked this. He had to hold back from snapping *"Now what?"* at her. There was obviously something going on with her.

There was always something going on.

"Your dad says he'll pick you up after ice dancing," Sander told Ello in the minivan the following morning.

Ello didn't reply, as if having a conversation with an old man would violate the rules of being a teenager.

"I haven't given you much reason to even want to talk to me, I guess," Sander said with a sigh.

Ello stared at him, nonplussed.

"Hey, Winstead, how you doing?" Sander hailed his dog in the rearview mirror. Winstead glanced at him from the third seat, then went back to sentry duty, watching out the side window for squirrel threats.

"I want to quit ice dancing," Ello blurted.

Sander glanced at her in surprise. "Really? But you've been doing it since you were little. You're really good."

Ello was shaking her head. "All my friends quit a long time ago. It's no fun anymore."

"I see," Sander replied reflectively as they paused at a light. "I guess I know what that's like. I used to play poker the first Thursday of every month with the same group of guys, but then so many of them retired and moved, and Jeff had a heart attack. . . . Pretty soon I stopped going. Then your grandma died. . . ." Sander's voice trailed off.

They drove in silence for a few minutes. "I just don't know how to tell Dad," Ello fretted. "He'll be so disappointed."

Sander mulled this over. "You're right. Your father is really proud of you. But parents have to adjust to all sorts of changes as their kids grow older. Would you like me to tell him?"

Ello stared at him in surprise. He interpreted her astonishment to mean, *Grandpa Sander's actually good for something?* He bit back the defensive retort that rose to his lips.

She had a point.

Ewan said, "Baba air wook la wa-faa!" and the twins exploded into synchronized laughter. Sander looked to his granddaughter for translation.

"Ewan says your hair looks like a waterfall."

"I've not heard that before," he confessed.

Ello was grinning, and Sander grinned back. Then the smile dropped from her face.

"No," she sighed. "I'll tell Dad."

Waiting for her at the ice rink was one of the main reasons she wanted to give up her lessons: Mitch. Mitch was her age: a thin, inexpert skater who perpetually fixed her in a gaze so brooding it made her nauseated. He always wanted to partner with her, to the point that Mrs. Steigler, the instructor, often intervened to give Mitch other skaters to practice with. When Mitch watched Ello skate with anybody else, it was like he'd given up blinking.

Mitch's pale skin served to accent his black hair so starkly that it almost looked fake, like a toupee, or Mr. Potato Head's mustache. His eyebrows were absurdly thick and bushy. His coal-black eyes glowed as he wrapped an arm around her waist, preparing for a dance that was thankfully mostly Finnstep—an active, hopping routine the class had been working on. She wasn't up for a waltz today, and neither was Mitch—his fingers were trembling. While Mrs. Steigler moved down the line of skaters, assessing their postures, Ello could see an internal struggle playing out on Mitch's face as he worked up his courage.

*Oh no.*

"Hey, Ello," he blurted. "Would you . . ."

"My dad says I have to be outside for him to pick me up

immediately after class," Ello interrupted. Meaning, *I can't do whatever it is you're about to ask me to do.*

Mitch nodded, but she could tell from his hooded gaze that he was never going to give up on this.

Winstead wagged in noncomprehension when Daddy lifted first one twin and then the other out of the car seats and handed them over to a smiling woman who smelled a little like raw chicken. Then Winstead was alone in the minivan with Daddy, curled up on the far back seat, content.

He smelled the familiar scents of their street, and knew when they pulled into the driveway that they were home. Daddy steered the minivan into the garage and parked it next to his enshrouded automobile. Moments later, he opened the side door.

"Come on," Daddy urged. "Let's go, buddy."

Winstead realized he didn't really want to jump out. He could anticipate the pain in his joints when he landed on the cement floor of the garage. Also, as car rides went, this one had been a little disappointing; they'd never gotten out anywhere, and instead had depleted their supply of younger humans and returned home.

Winstead wagged, trying to communicate his happy contentment with the ride process. Wouldn't it be better if the two of them, dog and man, simply got back on the road?

"Hey," Daddy murmured softly. "You okay, buddy?"

Winstead heard the question in the words. He wagged again.

Grunting, Daddy climbed into the minivan and sat down next to his dog. He reached out and gathered Winstead into his arms, holding him as if the big dog were a puppy. "Do you want to take a minute?" he asked gently.

Winstead closed his eyes. He reflected on all the things that he loved—dinner, walks, car rides—but this was the best: being held and loved by this man.

"Are we near the end, buddy? Am I going to lose you, too?" Daddy whispered.

Winstead pressed his head against his person's chest.

"Oh, Winstead. You're a good, good dog. But if it's time, I understand. I do, buddy. You don't have to hold on for me. You're my best friend in the world, and I'll be seeing you soon . . . you and Mommy. You can go to her if you need to."

Winstead breathed in and out, held by Daddy, as happy as he'd ever been.

# CHAPTER THIRTEEN

Ello would have been horrified to realize that she was talking to herself, Just Like Her Mother, practicing what she would tell her friends. "So after my lesson, all these people were coming in for free skate where they just go around and around in circles in the rink, and I was waiting for my dad and he was supposed to pick me up but he didn't come. So then I texted him, but he didn't respond. So then I texted my grandpa, but he didn't answer either. And then my mom didn't answer, but she's still in the hospital, so maybe that's against the rules or something. And I'm like, OMG, nobody is going to pick me up? So I, like, waited for twenty minutes and finally decided, okay, fine, I'll walk All The Way Home. Which is more than two miles."

The air was cold enough that she needed to keep her hands in her jacket pockets, but the snow had been sparse thus far this winter and had been shoveled cleanly from the sidewalks. Her Sorel boots, a dark stone color with faux fur that frankly looked better on Brittne than on Ello, were more than adequate to keep her dry and warm. She walked with her back slightly bent, as if the weight of her skates in her backpack constituted a burden she almost could not bear. Every few minutes, she scanned her phone for a text, but found none—Brittne's blockade still held.

"The moment I turn eighteen I'm moving to California or New York or someplace. Anyplace *not* here." Traverse City was just a bad fit for Eloise Goss. The summers were great, like how she imagined Hawaii might be, but the winters were pure North Pole.

By then, Ello would have a Real Boyfriend.

Somebody like Sean O'Brien.

The puppy had no name because she was not old enough to understand the words that had been spoken to her thus far in her ten weeks of life. She understood moods, though—the moods of the people who had been taking care of her since she'd been taken away from her mother dog. She knew there was a man whose emotions ran dark and angry. The little boy who gave the puppy the most affection was afraid of this man. So was the woman who lived in the house, holding a baby during most of her waking hours. And so was the puppy. The man often yelled loudly at the little dog, communicating clearly that the puppy was not pleasing to the angry man. This had taught the puppy to cower.

Only a few moments ago, the puppy had been sitting in the boy's lap in the back seat of a car, her paws on the window as she watched the bewildering world pass by out-side the glass. The man was in front, and he said something sharp that caused the boy to flinch. The puppy hunkered down, feeling the man's anger and the boy's fear rising in-side the car. And then with a lurch, the puppy nearly fell to the floor. The man stepped out and came around and yanked open the door next to the little boy. For a brief mo-ment, the little boy's hands encircled the puppy as if to pro-tect her, but then the angry man took the puppy away and set her roughly on the ground. She heard banging sounds, and then the scent of the boy and the angry man abruptly left with the wind.

The puppy was utterly alone and afraid. She sniffed the ground carefully, searching for clues about what was hap-pening. She trotted across the cold ground and found a place to take cover under some high, dry shrubbery. As she shivered, the curled leaves of the foliage made a rattling sound.

She was quivering from her fear as much as from the frigid air.

A stranger, tall and big like the angry man from the car, strode by with his eyes on the ground. He did not glance at where the puppy was hiding in the bushes. The puppy did nothing but watch the man.

She was trembling and sad and confused.

And then she saw the girl.

The girl's head was down, looking at something in her hand, and she did not see the puppy, who emitted an involuntary whimper. When the girl was about to pass the hiding place, the puppy made a decision and exploded out from underneath the branches and galloped straight at the girl, who turned in surprise.

"A puppy!" she cried. She crouched and the puppy leapt straight into her arms, wiggling and licking, no longer afraid, no longer cold, no longer anything but joyous.

This was, the puppy now understood, why the man had pulled her off the boy's lap and left her on the ground and driven away. This was why the puppy had hidden in the bushes. It was to wait for this girl, and now that they were together, nothing scary or bad would ever happen again.

Ello barely had time to gasp before the wriggling puppy was in her arms. She couldn't help but laugh at all the squirming. "Where did you come from?"

The puppy looked up at Ello with solemn brown eyes framed by a white and brown mottled face. Ello didn't know anything about dog breeds, but even she could tell this puppy was a mix of short-haired breeds, with piebald fur and a face a bit like a golden's.

"Okay," she decided. She strode up the walk to the nearest house, mounting the wooden steps to the front porch and ringing the doorbell. "Is this where you live?" Ello whispered to the puppy. "You are *so* cute!"

The inner door was opened by a kindly older lady who

grinned at the little dog and then raised her eyes at Ello in benign noncomprehension.

"Is this your dog?" Ello asked. "She was in your yard."

The woman shook her head. "No, I've never seen that puppy before. What a cutie!"

"Maybe one of your neighbors . . . ?" Ello suggested, looking around the street.

The woman shook her head again. "I'd probably know if someone got a new puppy. I think she's got to be a stray. See? She doesn't have a collar."

Ello was holding her face away from the puppy's constant tongue assault. "She ran up to me from your bushes. I'm not sure what to do."

"You could call the pound," the woman conjectured. "Or maybe take out an ad in the newspaper?"

Ello tried to picture doing either one of those two things.

"I'll tell you what. I have a collar and a leash I bought for my cat a few years ago. She *hates* them. You can have them if you want. I'll bet the collar would fit this little pup."

Ello thanked the woman and accepted the gift, but having the puppy secured with a pink leash and collar didn't at all advance Ello's thinking on what she was supposed to do next.

The puppy didn't seem to know either. The little girl (*Girl?* Ello checked. *Yep, a girl.*) darted out to the end of the restraint and then fell down and twisted and yanked. Ello tried to lessen the impact on the dog's neck with some extra slack.

"Hey! It's okay!"

Eventually Ello scooped the little dog off the ground and carried her like a football. The puppy accepted this as completely normal.

Winstead was deep into a dreamless nap. He didn't register the sound of the front door shutting, nor of people moving in the house. Then his eyes snapped open as something deep and instinctive alerted him, his senses urgently warning that something was happening right *now*.

And then there was a dog on his head. Winstead lurched to his feet, staring in astonishment at the little puppy, who was leaping and writhing in front of him. Winstead lowered his nose to the area under the puppy's tail and the puppy promptly squirted urine on the floor, letting the older dog know that yes, she was a dog, and meant no harm. The puppy was licking Winstead in the mouth as Ello stepped into the room.

Daddy grunted.

"Oh, hi, Grandpa," Ello greeted him. "I didn't mean to wake you. The puppy just ran in here like she knew where she was going."

Winstead was still examining the scents of the new puppy, who was bursting with so much kinetic energy—rolling on her back and leaping up to kiss Winstead and bowing and twisting—that Winstead couldn't help but wag.

"You did not wake me up; I was reading," Daddy corrected her gruffly. He frowned at the little puppy. "Where did that come from?"

At the sound of Daddy's voice, the puppy turned and scampered over and tried to scramble up his pant legs. A moment later the puppy abandoned those efforts and shoved her nose under the bed, snorting and sniffing, her little tail twitching.

"She kind of followed me home from the ice rink," Ello answered. The collar and leash in her left hand strayed farther behind her back as she related this edited version of events.

"Well . . ." Daddy shrugged. "Obviously it can't stay here."

Hunter walked up behind his father, who seemed to react to the approach but didn't turn away from the sliding doors to the backyard.

"Hey, Dad."

Sander nodded and kept watching out the window. Hunter joined him. Ello and the twins were frolicking in the backyard with a small puppy and Winstead.

"I honestly thought Winstead was on his last legs, but look at him go." Sander chuckled. "The old boy's been running nonstop for half an hour."

"Whose puppy?" Hunter asked curiously.

Sander gave him a sidelong glance. "Yours."

"Sorry?"

"I guess the little dog followed your daughter home from ice dancing. She named it Ruby."

Hunter winced. "Ice dancing! I was supposed to pick her up."

Sander nodded dryly. "Yes, you were, and now you have a puppy named Ruby. She said she texted you."

Hunter, frowning, patted his back pocket. His frown deepened.

"Want me to try calling it?" Sander offered.

Hunter shook his head in defeat. "It's probably at work, on my desk."

"How's Juliana?"

"Same. Mostly just sleeping. Hey, I have to work tomorrow. If she's not better, can I leave you in charge? And Monday, if it comes to that? I think all she needs is rest."

Sander regarded his son searchingly. "Tomorrow is Sunday," he chided Hunter. "Your wife is in the hospital."

"I know. We've got a bunch of minor issues with some of the new furniture."

"You've been working practically twenty-four seven. Couldn't you maybe take a break?"

"We always knew we'd have some problems," Hunter said, almost ready to reveal how the furniture boxes had spread like a virus from the software developers to the implementers and the support staff. People had brought in cardboard from home, like it was take-your-appliance-box-to-work day. But standing in the wash of light from the backyard, Hunter saw his father as an old, ailing man who could barely cope with the weak demands of his own life, and he decided not to burden him with his personal problems.

"Well," Hunter remarked instead, "we obviously can't keep a puppy."

# CHAPTER FOURTEEN

Monday morning, Ruby was savagely attacking a plastic superhero from the twins' vast collection, tossing it up in the air and then cringing away from it when it fell back down toward her head—puppy dodgeball. The toy's superpower was to be chewed to death without changing expression.

Something magical had occurred, and now Ello put voice to it. "I love you, Ruby. I love you so much."

Ruby was too focused on inducing mayhem to look up. Ello wondered if the puppy even understood why everyone kept using the word "Ruby." She leaned down and the puppy grabbed a mouthful of hair and began yanking. "Dad says we need to find your owners," she whispered.

Ruby paused and gazed at Ello with such an open willingness to love that Ello scooped the little dog up and kissed her on the snout. "Oh, Ruby . . . can't I have this one thing?"

At school, her usual clutch of friends was not in its usual position. There was no sign of Brittne in the hallways. Ello's ears, attuned to the social buzz of the hallway the way sparrows stay alert for mating calls, perked up when she heard a chorus of boys call out, "Hey, Sean!"

"How's it going, Sean?"

"Sean. Hi."

Ello turned and tracked Sean O'Brien as he headed toward her, grinning. Of course: grinning. He was wearing a Batman T-shirt. Nobody she knew had worn a Batman T-shirt since sixth grade, but here he was, strolling down the hallway unselfconsciously, nodding at the guys calling his name.

"Hello, Ello," he hailed cheerfully, smiling knowingly at the rhyme.

She blinked. "How come all the guys seem to know who you are, all of a sudden?" It made her feel weird, almost hostile, for some reason.

Sean shrugged. "Oh, I guess because this weekend I went to the rink and tried out for the club team."

"The rink? You mean the skating complex? I was there this weekend."

"You were?" Sean beamed. "I was on the hockey side; were you doing free skating?"

"No, I was . . . I do ice dancing. I'm going to quit, though."

So that's how easy it was for guys? Sean went to one hockey practice and now he was like the Most Popular? Without any effort at all? Then he walked around in a grade-school T-shirt and the boys still thought he was cool?

Boys had it so easy. It was Completely Unfair.

"We should skate sometime," Sean suggested breezily.

Ello's heart jumped—wait, had he just asked her to hang out?

"So, you know that assignment?" Sean continued. "For English, where we each have to pick someone and write a biography about them? I was wondering, could we maybe write about each other?"

Like she could say no to anything he asked.

In English class, they sat face-to-face, leaning forward and speaking in low tones over the buzz of all the other students doing their own interviews.

"My dad travels, like, all the time," Sean advised. "I was living with him, and then I had someone who would come over and stay with me when he was out of town, even though I'm fourteen. And then my mom is the head of her company. She works all the time. So, it's the same deal, only now she comes home at night and asks how my day went, like she's all of a sudden concerned about me." Something flickered in Sean's expression.

Ello wondered what to do—ask him about his parents' divorce? Tell him her own father and mother seemed to be headed down the same road? No, none of that felt right. She nodded, taking a different route. "I know. My dad works all the time too. Like, you know how long it's been since we had a vacation?" While she spoke, Ello was conscious of Sean's seemingly accidental examination of how she looked in her sweater. She felt her face warming under the scrutiny. Sean clearly liked this outfit better than her father did.

"My dad's really into football," Sean resumed. "My mom hates it, though. And then there's hockey. That's my favorite.

Mom doesn't like that either." Sean dropped his gaze to the list of suggested questions on the paper in front of him. "Okay, most prized possession?"

Ello thought about that. "Well, when I was little, my hero was this famous ice dancer, Meryl Davis."

Sean brightened. "Yes!" he replied, so enthusiastically that it unnerved her.

Yes *what*, exactly?

"So," Ello continued cautiously, "I saw her in the 2010 Olympics, when I was like four years old, and that's what I wanted to be from then on. An ice dancer. So Dad wrote her and she sent me a letter and a signed photograph. We had them in these frames in my bedroom—you know the kind that sit side by side?"

Sean cocked his head and regarded her with intense blue eyes that seemed to absorb her words with a disconcerting insight. "You said you 'had' them? What happened?"

"So, we had to move once the twins were able to stand up. The bedroom was too small for me to share with them. I think my parents were worried I'd strangle them in their sleep."

Sean laughed.

Ello noticed a few of the girls cut their eyes at him for a moment when he stretched his arms. "So we bought this bigger house," she continued. "Which was good until the room we called "Ello's Room" became my grandpa's room after Grandma died."

"I am so sorry," Sean consoled.

Ello paused, wondering if he was talking about her

grandma or the loss of a bedroom. "So anyway, the picture got misplaced." She shrugged. "Not that big a deal. Happened in the move. My dad never found his golf clubs."

"No, don't say that. . . . It must have been really bad," Sean protested.

Ello gave another shrug. "I'm not so much into it anymore."

"My aunt's an ice-dancing coach," Sean volunteered after a moment.

"I know, you told me. It's funny . . . most people don't even know what ice dancing is. They think it's figure skating."

"Well, I know the difference," he told her. "Why are you thinking of quitting?"

"I don't know," she replied. *I sound like an idiot.*

"My aunt taught me a few moves," Sean confided. "I'm probably nowhere near as good as you, though."

Ello felt herself blushing, and looked down at her paper to evade his eyes. "What about your most treasured possession?"

"Do you know who Wayne Gretzky is?"

Ello shook her head. "Who is he?"

"Oh my God. Only like one of the greatest hockey players in the history of the game. He had the most career goals, like 3,239."

"So you don't know the exact number?"

Sean blinked. Then he got it, and there was a different sort of appreciation in his eyes. He chuckled delightedly. "Anyway, I have one of his jerseys. Like, one he actually wore and signed. It's in my room in Detroit for when I go visit my dad." Sean paused. "Wow. So we both like sort of the same thing, the same most valuable objects!" He looked astonished, as if they'd just discovered they were from the same small town in Poland. She couldn't help but laugh at this boy. He reminded her of Ruby, bursting with puppy personality.

But then, as they stopped laughing, their eyes locked, and Ello's heart beat so loudly she was afraid he'd hear it.

# CHAPTER FIFTEEN

Apparently Mom was still in the hospital, because when Ello spotted the minivan, her grandfather was behind the wheel. She frowned at the change in routine. Then, when she slid open the door, Ruby flew out and straight into Ello's arms and the frown vanished. "Ruby!" She slid into her seat, holding the wriggling puppy in her lap. "Oh, you silly girl."

"I took her to see the vet at Petco," Grandpa told her. "He said Ruby is some sort of spaniel mixed with Labrador. Looks like she's about ten or twelve weeks old. Good health. Not microchipped. Winstead had his teeth cleaned. I'm going to drop you off at the house and then take the twins with me to the park and let everybody run around."

Ello peered at her grandfather. "Did you, like, have a lot of coffee or something?"

Sander grunted uncomfortably. "Just pitching in."

Ruby would just not stop kissing her, and soon Ello was giggling, her eyes scrunched shut under the assault. "Oh, Ruby, I love you so much." She noticed her grandfather regarding her with a peculiar expression. "What is it, Grandpa Sander?"

"I'm just reminded that you and your dad agreed you'd try to find Ruby's rightful owner. Are you doing that?"

Ello ignored the question, burying her face in puppy.

❄️

The next day, Tuesday, after picking the twins up from preschool, Sander sat by himself on a bench in the park and watched as Ewan and Garrett climbed the play structure and then tried to push each other off the top. The kid's area was separated from the dog park by a chain-link fence, so Sander could keep an eye on the twins and also Ruby and Winstead, the only two canines in the enclosure, wrestling and playing.

The sun was peering wanly out from behind thin gray clouds, the air still, and the play structure populated by several other small children who were eyeing the twins with reserve. Ewan looked around for something to throw at them.

Four women were seated across the park on their own bench, chatting and watching the children clamber up and down the ladders and slides. He noticed them noticing him. They were clearly nonplussed at his appearance. They seemed to reach a conclusion and rose in unison, marching over to see why he was trespassing. Two of the women were slim and slightly built with long brown hair—mother and daughter, Sander decided.

The daughter seemed to be in her thirties. "Hi," she greeted him. "Those your boys?"

Sander shrugged. "I'm their grandpa, but I can't be held legally responsible."

"How old are they? Twins, right?"

"Yes, identical. They are three. Three going on Seal Team Six."

The women laughed. "I'm Audrey, and this is my mom Allison," the daughter told him. Sander stood and introduced himself to all of them.

The family resemblance between Audrey and Allison went all the way down to the indistinguishable handshakes—small-boned fingers slipping weakly into his grip. The other two women were sizing him up, and one (he already couldn't remember her name) told him he was nice to bring the kids to the park ". . . and give your wife a break."

Sander nodded. "Actually, my wife died a little more than two years ago."

The women glanced at each other in something that looked like alarm. "Oh, so sorry," Audrey murmured. She nodded at Allison. "Mom's a widow."

"About four years ago," Allison added.

"Sorry for your loss," Sander replied automatically.

"So's my mom," announced the woman with a name that Sander thought was Sheri. Or Mary. Or Wanda. He looked at her. "A widow, I mean," she elaborated.

"My mom's a widow too," the last woman stated for the record. "She's really lonely."

Sander didn't know what to say to that.

Audrey sat on the bench, virtually pulling her mother

onto it with her. Sander realized that, if he sat, there wouldn't be room for the other two women, who were standing uncertainly, so he remained standing. "Oh, please, please, sit." He gestured to the bench.

Garrett leapt from the play structure and landed in the mud in the manner of a man whose parachute hadn't opened. Ewan jumped but missed his brother by inches. They both scrambled to climb back up and give it another try.

"Are you new to Traverse City?" Sheri/Mary/Wanda asked.

"Oh, no. I moved here after Barbara died."

More glances of obscure but certain significance were exchanged between them.

Sander didn't ask but found out that Allison loved to cook, did yoga, liked real books not ebooks, and lived in one of the large old houses off Front Street.

"Do you come to the park much? We haven't seen you," the other woman asked (Kay something? Kayla? Kate?).

"I've just recently decided to pitch in with the boys."

"Will you be here tomorrow?"

"Probably not. The nanny'll have the kids after preschool. I might come the day after, though." He cupped his hands around his mouth and shouted at the twins to stop braining the other kids with pine cones and to stop pouring dirt down the slide and for Ewan to find his missing shoe.

"I'll bring my mom with me next time," Kayla/Kate said.

Allison frowned at this. "Lucille wouldn't like it here in the park," she asserted.

For some reason, the Wanda-woman laughed.

"Oh stop," Kayla/Kate said.

"She wouldn't want to get mud on her shoes," Allison insisted.

It was, Sander concluded, a conversation he couldn't possibly participate in. He cleared his throat. "Very nice meeting you," he told them formally.

"Nice meeting *you*," Audrey responded with odd vehemence.

"See you day after tomorrow," Wanda/Suzette/Olga advised. "Thursday."

Kay/Kate/Katrina just smiled.

❄

Ello had been giving Ruby little nudges with her stockinged feet as they sprawled on the bed together, but now regretted it because the puppy had decided her toes were chew toys and was attacking them with sharp little teeth.

"Ow!" Ello called out sharply. Ruby stared, stunned, turning her head slightly. She was simply The Cutest Dog In The Universe. "Here, silly," Ello invited, dragging a dry washcloth across the comforter. Ruby pounced, biting the square of cotton in the jugular and shaking it viciously.

"Whoever had you didn't even get you a collar. They don't *deserve* you," Ello told the pup. "I just need for Mom to come home and meet you. Dad does whatever Mom says."

Her phone chirped with a text.

SW: Loved your outfit today!

It was Soffea, her message encrusted with emojis.

Ello paused, contemplating. She and Soffea had not texted in some time. Ello's choice. Well, Brittne's, really. What was the significance of this communication now, out of the blue? Was Soffea aware of the ruling by the queen of middle school and deliberately choosing to ignore it?

Ello swallowed. Soffea had never been anything but nice to her.

EG: Thanks!

Ello added a heart, a kiss, and a smiley face with hearts for eyes.

SW: OMG your B/F is so CUTE!!!!! 6Y*!

(*Sexy!)

That felt like an earthquake. Ello's thumbs hovered over the keys.

EG: He's not.

SW: W@? Oh YES he is!

EG: No I mean he's not my B/F.

SW: I thought he was visiting from another school. Someone said Croatia?

EG: No he lives here now. NUB.*

(*New Person.)

SW: OMG

EG: Did he say something about me?

SW: No I just thought so. NVM*

(*Never mind.)

Later, after she had put her phone down, Ello wondered why Soffea's comment had delivered such a shock to her inner San Andreas . . . what felt *different* about Sean, different

from other boys Ello had flirted with and crushed on . . .
but in the end, she decided IDK.*

(*I don't know.)

Sander awoke with a start. His son, barely illuminated in
the light from the hallway, was leaning over him, his face
completely in shadow.

"Dad," Hunter said softly. "That was the hospital calling.
I have to go back up."

Sander had not heard the phone ring. He rubbed his
face. "Time is it?"

"A little after four."

Sander sifted through Hunter's tone and detected raw
fear. For some reason, he felt compelled to reach out and
grab Hunter's hand, as if they were closing a business deal.
"You go on," Sander urged. "I can handle everything here."

As soon as Hunter left the room, Sander whispered,
"Oh, Barbara," and knelt next to his dog, spilling tears into
Winstead's fur.

At breakfast, it seemed that Sander had everything under control. The twins were reasonably clean and free of
most smears and crumbs when he dropped them off at preschool. Ello's slouching, burdened walk up her school steps
somehow looked less dreary and obdurate to him today.
Winstead and Ruby wrestled tirelessly in the back seat. The
nanny, Mrs. Espinoza, had preschool pickup duty, which gave
him freedom to do what he wanted. He debated heading over

to the park to see if Audrey and her mother were there, but in the end chose to drive down to the boardwalk along the bay to exercise the dogs, which gave his arm a workout as the puppy yanked and lunged on her leash. He was amused to see that whenever Winstead lifted his leg, Ruby would sniff and then squat in the same place. It was as if Winstead was giving Ruby dog lessons.

The dogs were out in the backyard, napping, when Sander left to pick up his granddaughter. He asked her if she'd like to get some ice cream, like the two of them used to do when he visited back in the day . . . back when Barbara was alive. Ello plainly didn't want to, but nodded anyway. Being an old widower gave him an advantage in these sorts of negotiations.

Hunter was waiting for them in the kitchen by the time they returned home. He was holding a glass of amber liquid. Sander stared; Hunter seldom drank, and certainly not in the afternoon. Ello sensed something too, evident in the stiff way she halted when she saw her father.

"I need to talk to you," Hunter said gravely.

# CHAPTER SIXTEEN

What Hunter needed to do more than anything was start speaking right now, because Ello was regarding him with a gouging terror. The problem was, he didn't trust his voice not to crack, and if he let his daughter see his own fear, it might kill her.

Sander's face betrayed nothing but grim purpose, ready to hear the absolute worst. Even the dogs seemed anxious, though they displayed it in different ways: Winstead was focused and tense, while Ruby had put her bottom on the floor and was wagging a tiny bit, just a flutter, carefully watching Ello.

Hunter took a deep swallow of his whiskey, some irrelevant part of his brain pondering why it was that in the movies alcohol seemed to bring resolve and steadfastness to a person, whereas all it did to Hunter was blast an unnerving ball of fire into his stomach.

"Dad?" Ello asked tremulously. She reached down, scooped up Ruby, and clutched the little puppy to her chest.

"Ello . . ." Hunter began. "There is no easy way to say this."

Ello cringed.

"Your mother is in organ failure."

Sander reacted to this news with a widening of his eyes, but Ello shook her head frantically. "Wait, what does that mean? Organ failure?"

"It means that her infection is so bad it's invading her vital organs. The doctors have put her into a coma to keep her stable, and they're doing the best they can. I came home to get you. Mrs. Espinoza is taking the boys home with her. Let's put the dogs in the basement. There's nothing a puppy can destroy down there." He set the whiskey glass down on the coffee table. "Let's go."

Ello thought she was ready. While in the car, she mentally prepared herself for what she'd encounter in the hospital, telling herself she would be strong and brave for her family. But when she saw her mother lying in bed connected to all the tubes and the machines, olive-complexioned face somehow turned *pale,* Ello crumpled. Only her father's swift movement to embrace her kept her from dropping to the floor.

"Ello. Ello," her father murmured.

She gripped him and concentrated on trying to find strength. Finally she wiped her eyes and raised them to her father. "Could I have a few minutes to talk to her alone?"

Sander and Hunter glanced at each other, communicating something; then, with a nod, they left the room.

Ello reached out and took her mother's listless hand. "Mom," Ello whispered.

For a moment that was all she could manage, that one word. Then she swallowed, shaking her head. "Mom, please, I can't lose you. I can't imagine life without you. The whole family needs you, Mom," Ello pleaded. She was crying now: choking, gasping sobs that made it difficult to speak or even breathe.

"I am so sorry. I'm sorry I've been such a bitch. I mean, I don't know why . . ." Ello trailed off. "Mom, please come home. Please get better. I promise if you do, I won't act the way I've been acting. I'll clean up my room. I'll do my homework. And I'll make sure that Ruby gets back to her owner."

Ello leaned over and pressed her face into her mother's shoulder and her throat constricted agonizingly, as if it were tearing apart. "Just don't die, Mom! Please! Please!"

Sander and Hunter found a cold, sterile room with coffee and couches and no comfort. They went to the coffee cups automatically, but in the end, Hunter declared that his sour stomach wouldn't let him contemplate drinking any more of the stuff. He gestured for Sander to partake if he wanted, but Sander wasn't interested either.

Sander stared at his pain-wracked son, feeling utterly helpless. Surely there was something he could do. But Hunter was looking deep inside himself and seemed to have forgotten there was anyone else in the room.

Sander wondered when his son and he had last exchanged a hug. Not the back-thumping, awkward embrace when they'd been separated for a while and were saying hello, but a real, loving hug. A father embracing his boy. A boy who needed his dad. Had to be back when Hunter was twelve or so. After that, he was too grown-up. A father didn't force that sort of affection on a son once the boy got to a certain age—right? Or should Sander have insisted on it for himself?

He knew he should utter something comforting, and he groped for the words. An alarming sadness was building up inside him, some unexpressed grief determined to volcano its way to the surface. He had spent so much time in hospitals while Barbara struggled. The smells and sounds were sickeningly familiar and gave him vertigo.

Sander tamped down the unexpected surge of emotion. *This isn't about you, it's about your son.*

"Hunter."

Hunter looked at him with dead eyes.

"I just want you to know that, if the worst thing happens, if we lose Juliana . . . No, no, wait, listen. I'm saying that when your mom died, I thought the world had ended. And, though sometimes it still feels like it did, I'm still alive, I'm still living life. I have you and my grandchildren. We can get through it together. We'll still have life, and life goes on."

Hunter shook his head, a pitying look on his face. "No, Dad," he grated in strangled tones. "Without Juliana, there *is* no life."

Sander drove with his granddaughter in the seat next to him, Hunter remaining back at the hospital.

Ello's expression resembled her father's: a dead stare into an abyss. Suddenly she turned to Sander as if on the attack, her eyes sparking hard at him. "As soon as I get home, I'm going online. I'll post those pictures of Ruby. And I'll call the, the animal rescue whatever, and I'll have Ruby picked up. She'll have a better chance of finding her family if she goes to the shelter."

Sander took in her sudden intensity. He gave it a few beats. "I think with all that's going on, maybe this isn't the best time. Your puppy's not a burden—in fact, Winstead seems so full of spunk and energy right now, it's the opposite, it's a gift. And maybe you could use someone to sleep on your bed and snuggle with you, a friend you can count on."

Ello gaped at him in wonder.

Sander shrugged. "I'll tell your dad, if you want. I just think we need Ruby right now."

Ello had thought she was all cried out, but Grandpa's unexpected kindness put tears in her eyes. Sander reached out and placed a reassuring hand on her arm.

The next morning, Ruby was alerted to something, a change in the electric charges in the air. Curious, she abandoned her quest to find edible objects among the scatterings in the boys' room and trotted out to investigate.

She found Winstead alertly watching the bathroom door in Sander's bedroom. It was from Winstead that Ruby had detected the change in emotion. Ruby sniffed Winstead, who ignored her.

For Ruby, every single day was a novel experience, so she assumed there was some vitally important reason why Winstead was standing sentry outside the door. When she pounced on the older dog's foot to try to inject even more joy into the situation, Winstead shook her off in irritation.

Winstead and Ruby both wagged when the bathroom door opened.

"What do you two want?" a dripping, betoweled Sander demanded gruffly.

In the kitchen, Ruby watched Winstead for clues on how to behave in this room of amazing odors. The old man struggled with the two boys, finally managing to jam them into their high chairs. When Ello entered, Ruby bounded joyously over to greet her. Ello stooped and allowed the puppy kisses for a moment or two, then stood up.

Ello examined what Sander had placed on the twins' trays. "Peanut butter, toast, chocolate milk," she observed neutrally.

Sander shrugged. "Well, I burned the pancakes and then I thought, what's a pancake but a form of bread? And then, you put butter on it. What's wrong with peanut butter?" He grinned at her triumphantly.

Ello slid into her chair. "Uh-huh."

Now Ruby realized why the old dog had taken up a position between the two high chairs. As the boys made noise, gurgling and laughing, they dropped a steady shower of bits of food from above—a treat-rich environment. Ruby eagerly darted forward and snapped up a piece of bread crust, and Winstead gave her a surly look.

"What about your fried eggs?" Ello challenged him.

"Peanut butter toast is fine for me. What'll you have, Ello?"

Ruby knew who "Ello" was. She raised her eyes and gazed lovingly at her girl.

"Why not toast," Ello decided. "Oh! With *strawberry jam.*"

"That's the spirit," Sander praised. For just a moment they were smiling at each other, and then Ello's face went cold. Ruby, sensing something, went to Ello's chair and tried to climb up in her lap. Already she understood that her purpose was to keep her girl happy. After a moment, Ello reached down and picked her up, and the little dog felt some of her girl's sorrow melt away.

Ello thought she had perfected the iron mask with which she could face down the world. When she set her expression a certain way, no one could see her feelings, because she was keeping them tightly under wraps. It was the best defense she had against being an eighth-grade girl. But what nearly broke her was the car ride to school.

Sander was chatting joyfully without seeming to notice that his granddaughter had lapsed into a sullen silence. How could he act so happy? Did he think it was his job to try to cheer her up? With Mom in the hospital?

The twins, responding to Grandpa's energy, were in high spirits, kicking and laughing and babbling. Periodically, her grandfather asked her for a translation, which she provided reluctantly, resenting that she even *had* brothers. She felt like turning and belting both of them. She Felt Like Screaming.

Of course the twins did not understand anything. They had not seen their mother lying there nearly dead, poked full of holes, tubes and cables trailing from her like an external circulatory system. They didn't know that this might be the new family: Sander, the children, Hunter at work, no mom.

Ello held it together because the last thing she wanted was for her grandfather to start hugging her or something. She needed to keep this locked up and deal with it without interference from adults. She needed her *friends*.

But, of course, the legs had been knocked out from under her support system. Brittne was isolating Ello, and everyone in their group followed Brittne's lead. Which Was Stupid. Ello recalled how many times she had frozen out a person because it was what Brittne wanted. Her stomach heaved at the memories.

She may have been aware of Brittne or Mourgen in the hallway, but did not look at them or acknowledge they existed. They were Acting So Middle School.

She would have said hi to Soffea, but she was looking for one person only, and when she saw him she strode straight up to him.

His face registered his alarm as she approached. "What happened?" he asked.

Ello couldn't help herself, couldn't stop the tears as she told him.

"Is she going to be okay?" Sean asked her urgently.

*Okay.* What a word. How do you get from being in organ failure to anything resembling *okay*?

Ello couldn't reply, but Sean didn't seem to require an answer. He held out his arms and gathered her so gently, so respectfully, and yes, so lovingly, that for the first time since hearing the words "organ failure" she felt taken care of. As she pressed her face into his shirt, she was aware of how quickly she was soaking it with tears.

"No public displays of affection," the history teacher, Mr. Morrison, lectured as he passed by.

When neither Sean nor Ello broke the embrace, Mr. Morrison halted, a stern expression on his face. "Did you hear me? No public displays of affection. Break it up. Now."

Sean made no move to obey. "It's not affection, dickhead," he retorted. "It's humanity."

Mr. Morrison stiffened. "You just earned yourself a trip to the vice principal's office, young man. Let's go."

And Sean did go, but not just then. He gave it another minute or so, letting Ello recover so that she wouldn't be bawling when they parted. As Sean followed the history teacher down the hall, Ello watched him in wonder.

# CHAPTER SEVENTEEN

I t was the second time Thursday had rolled around since Thanksgiving, which meant no Mrs. Espinoza, which meant Sander would be picking up the boys if they survived another day at preschool without injury or arrest. The forecast called for snow, but the gray, pregnant clouds were withholding. It seemed like a perfectly normal thing for Sander to take the dogs to the park where he had met Allison and her daughter, Audrey. In fact, their last conversation had seemed to imply to Sander that he had something like a reservation.

When he clanged the gate on the dogs, he turned and regarded the preschool-aged children on the playground equipment. They looked familiar. He also recognized their moms: what's-her-name and whatever-her-name-was, plus Allison (sans daughter Audrey) and two other women who looked to be in their early sixties, maybe. Every single one of them waved, so he had no choice but to walk over.

"This is the woman I was telling you about. Claire, this is Sander," one of the moms said. He couldn't see the family resemblance. Claire had thick hair with a hint of red in it—there was a name for that color that Barbara had tried and failed to teach him—and her brown eyes seemed a tad mischievous as she shook his hand.

"Sander, as in the machine? Or is it short for something?" Claire asked him.

"Short for something? Like what?" he asked without thinking. He had the sense he had been rude, but . . . well, too late.

Claire was unoffended. "I don't know. Salamander?"

Sander laughed. The other women looked a little impatient.

"This is my mom, Lucille," one of the younger women told Sander.

Lucille's expression was challenging and assessing as she scoped Sander up and down. Her DNA matched her daughter's—blue eyes, blond hair, and skin that was probably pale but looked incongruously tanned despite the time of year. Lucille was what Sander's father used to call a "full-figured gal," dressed in a formfitting winter coat and tall boots—what Barbara would have termed "stylish." Her grip was the most firm of all the women's. "Nice to meet you, Lucille."

"I'm Allison," Allison stated, sounding defensive.

"Yes, I remember; nice to see you again, Allison."

Okay, too many names to remember. Allison . . . she was thin and straight as an alley. Alley Allison. Claire had clear eyes and clear, glowing skin. Clear Claire. Alley Allison, Clear Claire, and Lucille . . . Lucille wasn't Allison or Claire.

Allison passed a hand through her thin brown hair, glaring at Lucille for some reason. "It's supposed to snow again," she declared after a moment.

"So you're the famous Sander Goss," Lucille observed with a throaty laugh.

"Famous?" Sander repeated.

"We could all sit down if we went to the picnic table," Claire said. Clear Claire.

Everyone but Allison smiled and nodded.

"The seats are metal. My butt will freeze," Allison pouted.

"Well, I don't have to worry about that," Lucille chortled, giving her rear end a slap. "Natural padding."

Allison bit her lip and glanced away.

Sander looked between the two women, then to Claire, who was giving him a knowing smile.

"You seem bemused, Sander," Claire stated lightly.

They settled around an octagonal, metal-mesh picnic table. "Bemused?" Sander asked, turning the word over in his mind.

"You don't seem to have grasped the impact that an appearance of an eligible bachelor like you might have on women of a certain age and status in this area," Claire continued. Clear Claire providing Clarification.

Allison was gaping at Claire. Sander wondered what his own expression looked like.

"You are certainly an attractive man," Lucille added, meeting Sander's gaze directly and unwaveringly.

"God, Lucille, you're just so obvious about everything," Allison complained.

"What do you mean, Allie?" Lucille asked mildly. "Don't you think Sander is handsome? Or have you always worn mascara to the playground?"

Sander looked between the women, baffled. Claire had her eyebrows raised at him, as if asking a question he hadn't heard. The younger women were glancing at each other with ill-concealed enthusiasm for whatever was going on.

Allison crossed her arms over her chest. "Where are your boys today, Sander?"

"Oh. They're at preschool. I'll head back to pick them up pretty soon."

"They are so *cute*," Allison informed Lucille and Claire. "So full of energy. I just love children." This last statement was directed at Lucille, and seemed almost like an attack. For some reason, it made Claire grin.

Lucille waved off the comment. "Allie thinks because I have a place in Florida where I escape the winter that I don't love my grandkids."

"That's ridiculous," Lucille's daughter declared bluntly, her blue eyes flashing.

"I never said anything like that!" Allison retorted.

"Don't you get sick of winter sometimes, Sander?" Lucille asked huskily.

It almost seemed to Sander that she was asking something else entirely, but he couldn't at all comprehend what. He glanced at Claire, who continued watching him knowingly, as if they shared a secret.

Somehow Ello slogged through the rest of the school day, enduring the lectures and the assignments. Not one of her classmates, not even those who seemed to understand that she and Brittne were on the outs, had a single thing to say to her, though it had to be obvious that Something Was Very Wrong in her life. No one asked if she was okay or expressed any concern that she was being so quiet. It was as if, at this stage of life, when an eighth-grade girl was grappling with something far more important than the usual social dramas, no one had the emotional fortitude to address it. Easier to pretend Ello wasn't there, wasn't sitting with her head bowed, staring at her open math book without seeing it.

She caught her teachers watching her sometimes and wondered if Sean had confided in the vice principal, who had tipped off the staff to her mom's illness, but the teachers either respected her privacy or were as oblivious to her emotional state as the students.

And Sean . . . since the incident with Mr. Morrison that morning, he'd vanished from the halls as if plucked from the planet by a UFO. Ello felt responsible—she'd gotten him in trouble, and who knew what fate had befallen him? She itched to text him, but hesitated due to her sense of guilt over the situation.

After school, Sander was right where he should be, parked in the pickup zone when Ello extracted herself from the school building. She opened the door of the minivan and gasped in shock. "What happened?"

The boys had each been on the receiving end of a haircut, shaved close on the sides and a little long on top. Sander had been to the barber too, though his white hair wasn't styled any differently, just shorter: no longer woolly and wild, no longer springing out over his ears and curling up on the back of his neck.

"Mom takes them for haircuts," Ello seethed. "You should have waited for *Mom*."

Sander regarded her intently. Some sort of understanding passed behind his green, Ello-like eyes. He nodded. "You're right, Ello," he agreed. "I am so sorry. I figured it had been so long since I had gotten my own hair chopped, I might as well take the boys with me."

Ello wasn't mollified. "Are you going to, like, change everything now? Like you're our new mother?"

"No. Oh no, Ello, not at all. I'm just helping until she gets better," Sander assured her.

"Because she is going to get better," Ello insisted sternly.

"Right. Of course."

But she was still angry at him.

After playing with Ruby for half an hour or so at home, Ello curled up in her bed and grabbed her phone. A text awaited from Sean.

SOB: Hey.

Thumbs flying, Ello texted back.

EG: Hey! What happened? After you went down the hall with Mr. Morrison you weren't in class.

SOB: I got suspension for 3 days.

EG: W@????

SOB: It was for using inappropriate and sexually suggestive words. They gave me a pass on the PDA.

EG: IMSS.* (*I'm so sorry.) It's my fault.

SOB: What? No, it was Morrison's fault. They asked me

why I called him a dickhead and I said it was because he was being a dickhead.

EG: LOL.

SOB: My mom is freaking out. Really pissed at me.

EG: Sorry.

SOB: I'm not.

Ello froze at those words. Was he saying he was not sorry that he had called a teacher a dickhead? Or was he not sorry that he hugged her? Or was he not sorry that it was seen by others as a public display of affection?

Ello desperately wanted to know, so she changed the subject.

EG: Do you want me to collect your homework or something?

SOB: No, that's OK, they said they would email it.

Ello was disappointed.

Later she and Ruby snuck into her parents' bedroom, creeping like house burglars. Her mom's desk in the corner was a sanctum, a place where all her lists and reminders dwelled. Ello simply wanted to touch something her mother had recently touched. But first she had to pull a slipper from her puppy's mouth. That done, she picked up a list from the desk, her eyes widening, but she was interrupted by Ruby, who squatted on the rug, and had to run the puppy outside.

At dinner, Ello told her grandfather, "You do know there's a difference between cooking and reheating, right?"

Sander accepted this with a chuckle. "Okay," he agreed. "Tomorrow, I'll cook. Or, how about this: we'll both cook."

Ello nodded skeptically. "Sure."

"I used to make a mean chili, though it was more mean than chili."

Ello had No Idea What He Was Saying. "Okay," she declared, unfolding the piece of paper. "I found this." She gave her grandfather her most defiant glare.

Sander craned his neck, trying to read the small writing. "What is it?"

"Mom's Christmas to-do list. We need to do everything it says."

Sander nodded thoughtfully. "Okay, kiddo."

"She would hate if she came home and we hadn't done anything."

"Sure."

"We don't even have a tree yet. That's just wrong."

Sander spread his hands. "It's only the fifth of December."

Ello bristled. "Mom would want a tree!"

Sander nodded, clearing his throat. "Your dad called. He says that your mom hasn't changed. But"—Sander leaned forward earnestly—"that's actually a good thing, Ello. The doctors told him it means there's been no deterioration in her condition. Right now, that's everything."

Ello nodded woodenly, remembering her mom in that hospital bed.

"Do you want to go see her? I'll drive you up anytime," Sander offered. "Mrs. Espinoza says she'll take the twin tornadoes."

Ello swallowed and shook her head. "I . . . can't," she said haltingly. "Is that bad? Do you think she knows I'm not visiting?"

After a moment of consideration, Sander shook his head emphatically. "No, not at all. When your grandma was like this, when she was fading in and out, I was always there. I never left her side. But then, when she rallied and we talked, she had no idea I'd been sitting in that chair the whole time. She said she wished I had done something else with my time. She was . . ." Sander's face froze, then pinched in on itself. "There she was with cancer in her liver, but all she cared about was me."

He bent forward, elbows on the table, and lowered his face into his open hands. Soon his shoulders were shaking. Winstead leapt to his feet and thrust his nose up toward Sander's face. Ello hurried around the table to her grandfather, throwing her arms around him and sobbing with him over loss and fear and loneliness.

All the twins could do was stare in shock.

Hunter sat by Juliana's side. She was absolutely motionless, but the electronics in the room were still flickering with glowing green numbers. So even if she didn't appear to be alive, she had to be. The machines said so.

"You don't have to worry about anything. It's all under control," Hunter murmured to her. Was it okay to lie to someone in a coma? In truth, the word that applied *least* to Hunter's life right now was "control."

He forced himself to stop thinking about it. "I remember when I saw you on campus the first time," he told her finally. "You were this amazing beauty. I figured out that you went to pick up your mail every day at the same time, so I'd park and watch you in my rearview mirror. Pretty quick I realized I couldn't come up with a single excuse to talk to you. Like, what was I going to say? 'How's your mail this morning? Any interesting letters?'" Hunter hunched forward. "Did I ever tell you that when I found out you were from Brazil, I went to the language arts building and asked if anyone taught a class in Brazilian? I wondered why they were looking at me like I was an idiot. Then someone finally said you spoke Portuguese. Oh, man. But when I found out you were in that club that went to hospitals and sang Christmas carols, I thought, that's it! I signed up, but I didn't know that because my voice was deep I wouldn't be able to stand next to you. So I sang loudly so you'd notice me. And it worked, because you looked at me and smiled!"

Hunter's phone vibrated, and when he looked down at it his smile faded.

It was a text from Valerie O'Brien.

VOB: Where are you? This is a critical time!

Hunter took several moments to compose his reply.

HG: Sorry, my wife is in organ failure and is comatose in the hospital. I should have let you know sooner, but I have been preoccupied.

Hunter wondered if the word "preoccupied" was too sarcastic, but he sent the message anyway. There was a long pause.

VOB: Any idea when you will be able to return?

Hunter stared at his phone.

HG: What kind of person would ask such a question at a time like this? Are you simply so awful you have no sense of any sort of common decency? My wife may be dead very soon. I should think you would care about an employee's personal tragedies at least to the point of expressing some sort of concern. You are not a human being.

Hunter regarded his message, heart pounding in his chest. At that moment, if Mrs. O'Brien had walked into the room, he would have punched her in the face.

After a long minute, Hunter erased his unsent text and typed another.

HG: Nobody knows.

# CHAPTER EIGHTEEN

A s a little girl, Ello had vehemently protested the idea that the Goss family would bundle up and head out to a choose-and-cut tree farm to pick a tree to whack down and decorate for Christmas. She couldn't bear the thought of an "innocent tree" being "murdered" so they could put it in their living room. So for years, they had come to this parking lot at Meijer Thrifty Acres to find a Scots pine that was already chopped down—or "pre-murdered," as Hunter had explained under his breath.

Mrs. Espinoza was feeding and bathing the twins and hopefully preventing them from throwing butcher knives at each other before bedtime, so only Sander and Ello and the dogs had set out to find this season's Christmas tree.

Ello trooped up and down the rows, stopping to examine and reject each one based on selection criteria only she understood. Winstead, less fussy, had already marked several he would be okay with. The puppy was alternately attacking pine branches and Winstead.

Sander slapped his hands together. It was cold out under the harsh lights. "What about that one?" he asked.

"Too sparse at the top," Ello replied dismissively.

"Looks okay to me."

Ello shot him a look. "You don't know my mother. It's got to be *perfect*."

Ello went back to her microscopic inspection of every pine needle and Sander watched her with a slight frown on his face. "There's no cause and effect, Ello," he finally ventured.

"What do you mean?"

"A perfect tree won't make your mother get better."

She scowled. "I know that," she snapped. "I'm not a child."

He held up his hands in surrender. "Okay."

"God."

"I'm sorry."

She stabbed a finger at a specimen that was, as far as Sander could determine, no different from any other. "This one," she declared.

The man running the operation billowed bourbon fumes as he cheerfully pulled a tag from their selection and went to ring it up. Sander followed, fingering his wallet. Ello scooped Ruby off the ground.

They stood at a checkout stand fashioned from plywood and sawhorses while the professional tree seller punched at an iPad, frowning and shaking his head. "That's not right," he lectured his electronics.

"What are those?" Ello asked.

Everyone but Winstead looked where she was pointing. Behind them stood a stack of objects in burlap—they looked a bit like corpses to Sander. He wasn't sure he wanted to hear bourbon-breath's answer.

"Oh, we ordered too many trees this year. Those are the extras." He went back to thumbing the iPad.

"You're just going to throw them away?" Ello demanded, sounding outraged.

The man shrugged, indicating he could only do one thing at a time here.

"We'll take that one."

Everyone, even the dogs, seemed startled.

The man frowned at her, then cast a glance at the tree mummies. "You want one of them?"

Sander noted the set to Ello's jaw. "How much?" he inquired, wallet out and ready.

The man scratched himself, evidently deciding it took all kinds. "Ten bucks?" he offered. Sander wordlessly offered two fives and the man stuck the bills in his pocket, bypassing the cash register. "You want help loading it up?"

With a belch that smelled like it had been aged in a barrel, the tree man carried the confined pine to their vehicle. The minivan filled with the redolence of pine. Winstead could not stop sniffing at this strange object that stretched from back door to dashboard.

"I want to apologize for what I said at the tree lot," Sander ventured.

Ello fixed him with a vulnerable gaze. "I don't think about it," she murmured.

"About . . . your mom's illness?"

She nodded, swallowing. "I have to force myself to believe it. Believe that she's sick, that she might die. Most of the time it's not real to me at all. I don't feel anything: not about Mom, not about anything else. I don't let myself feel anything."

Sander considered his reply. "That's called denial," he advised after a moment, not adding that it was also known as the first stage of grief. "It's a survival mechanism."

"I'm not a horrible person?" she whispered.

"Oh, Ello, no. No, of course not." Sander turned into a Walgreens parking lot and stopped the minivan. He faced his granddaughter and then faced his own wretched tragedy. "When your grandmother was first diagnosed, that first weekend, we never spoke of it." He closed his eyes briefly. He would *not* cry again over this in front of Ello. She needed to hear that grief was survivable. "We just went about our day. I was building a cabinet in the workshop and went out and lost myself in it. Hours went by and then I realized she was alone in the house. I raced in and she was folding laundry and singing to herself." Sander smiled at the memory. "The worst day of our lives, and we were happy because we were pretending that it wasn't true. No, Ello, denial is a way to stay positive. My advice is to hold onto it as long as you can."

Ello's expression was so adult in that moment that Sander almost forgot she was still a little girl, barely a teenager.

"Thanks, Grandpa."

The next morning, Saturday, Ello was critically examining her silhouette when she noticed Ruby, who was lying on the bed, raise her head. Then the puppy plunged off onto the floor and ran to the door, wagging, pressing her nose to the crack for a sniff. A huge answering snort came from the other side. Ruby scratched at the door.

"Winstead?" Ello wondered aloud.

A knock followed.

Definitely not Winstead. Ello cautiously opened the door and Sander was standing there. Winstead pushed past her legs and instantly was wrestling with Ruby in surprised delight, as if the two of them had never seen each other before.

"Grandpa? What are you doing upstairs?" she blurted without thinking.

He grinned at her. "I come up here sometimes."

"Huh." A thought struck her. "Like when I'm at school?"

"No," he laughed. "Are you almost ready to go?"

"Yeah, almost." She gestured him into her chambers and was relieved to see him glance around with a lack of familiarity. Okay, so he wasn't up here Going Through Her Things when she was away. *Ew.*

He cleared his throat. "I just wanted to thank you again for the fried eggs every morning."

She cocked her head at that, puzzled.

He shrugged, smiling sadly at himself. "Not just that. I realized recently that it's the one thing I look forward to all morning. Sometimes all day. You come in, and it's like Winstead when Ruby arrived. For a brief moment, you bring an energy I don't have myself."

Ello felt a flash of shameful self-loathing. She lowered her eyes to the floor. "I never talk to you."

"No, that's not right. You usually say something. And I get that I haven't been much fun to chat with lately. No, not just lately. . . . Ever. I've been feeling sorry for myself, and when a man is in that mood he's not of much use to anyone, including himself. You're not just my granddaughter, Ello. You're one of my best friends in the world."

Ello took a slow, deep breath. She stared at her grandfather, at his moist eyes and trembling smile, and suddenly found herself across the room and hugging him without realizing she'd even moved.

He gently patted her back.

They pulled out of the surprise intimacy and looked to the dogs as an escape from the awkwardness. Ruby, impossibly, had Winstead pinned to the floor and was mouthing the huge dog's throat.

"Who's this?" Grandpa asked, looking at Ello's collage of Brittne and Ello photos.

Of course he wanted to know who the girl with the huge brown eyes was. Even though the pictures were all from sixth and seventh grade, anyone could see that Brittne was a stunner.

"That's Brittne. We're kind of not talking to each other right now. It's . . . complicated."

He nodded, still examining the shots.

"I just have to get my stuff and we can go," Ello informed him a little impatiently.

"Did she pick out the photographs?" Sander asked.

"Yeah. She put it all together and framed it for my birthday."

Sander nodded. "Thought so."

"Sorry?"

He pointed to a picture of Ello and Brittne at the beach in Charlevoix. Then another on the Ironton Ferry. Then another, goofing off at Torch Lake. "She looks perfect in every single one."

"Well, yeah," Ello agreed, a bit bitterly. "Because Brittne *is* perfect. She always has been, even—"

"—But look at you," he interrupted, peering at a photo. "In this one, you're out of focus. This one, your hair's funny. This one doesn't look even look like you. In this one there's, what, a shadow across your face. She picked pictures to make you look bad." He regarded Ello mildly. "How long have you been friends?"

Sander was driving, Ello next to him in the passenger seat. The twins were occupied with a video on an iPad in the back. Ello decided not to mention how much Juliana loathed it when her children looked at screens instead of interacting with people. Ello's thumbs were flying on her phone, texting Soffea and another one of Brittne's exiles, Ashleigh. Turns out, She Had Friends. Maybe they had been there all the time, like the stars that only show up when the sun goes down.

"I don't know how you do that," Sander observed.

Ello blinked at him. "What?"

"I can't type on those things at all. The buttons are too small. Every word is a typo."

"Oh. Then just dictate," she suggested.

"Sorry?"

Ello thumbed her phone and held it to her face. "Hi Grandpa. This is Ello. I am sitting in the seat next to you. When you get this text, comma, you'll remember that you can just speak your messages into your phone."

"I'll be darned," Sander marveled as his phone beeped. "Thanks, kid."

"Technical support. . . . Isn't that why you have grandkids?"

Sander laughed and they drove on in silence for a moment. "Did you talk to your father yet? About quitting?"

Ello knew what he meant; they were on their way to her ice-dancing lesson. She shook her head. "The few times I've seen him since Mom went to the hospital, he's been totally wrecked, you know? I didn't think he could handle it."

Sander nodded. "He has a lot going on right now. Might be best to wait until he's out of the woods on all of that."

Ello regarded her grandfather in his new haircut and strange new role as her confidant and friend. "Is my mother going to die?" she asked bluntly.

Sander flinched, then gave her a solid look. "I don't think anyone expects that."

Ello blinked back her tears. Hearing his encouragement somehow made her want to cry more than contemplating the worst did.

"While you're at your lesson, I'll take the boys to the park," Sander told her. "And then when we're home, I'll take the dogs for a walk."

"Grandpa?"

Sander raised his eyebrows at her.

"Thank you for everything."

Sander was back at the house, preparing to take the dogs and boys to what he now thought of as Widow Park, when his phone chirped. It was a text from Allison. He no longer thought of her as Alley Allison because he'd spent a little time with her and could now tell her apart from Clear Claire and Not-Claire Lucille.

AT: Sander?

Sander raised the phone to his mouth and pressed the dictate button. "Hello Allison," he pronounced distinctly.

SG: Hello Allison.

He grinned, pleased with himself.

AT: How come you didn't call?

Sander frowned. When? Why was he supposed to call Allison?

SG: I did call, member? I told you how much I enjoined having coffee with you.

AT: Right but I thought you would be calling me again. When I didn't hear from you I thought I had done something wrong.

Sander took a deep breath.

SG: Sorry. No, hi horse not I am Ron, I am just sane I didn't have a reason Paul.

AT: What?????

SG: Not Paul! Paul! Paul! At sake!

AT: I don't know what you are saying!

She answered on the first ring. "I'm trying to use the phone to dictate texts," he explained by way of apology.

"Oh. I thought you were mad at me."

"No, of course not. I was explaining you didn't do anything wrong, I was just saying I didn't have a reason to call. Not Paul, call."

"Well, I'm very glad you called," Allison replied.

"Sure," he agreed. *Wait! Did I call?* "What's on your mind?"

"Sorry?"

"Why did you want me to call?" Sander elaborated.

"Oh. I just really enjoyed having coffee with you."

"Yes," Sander agreed. They had both said that already. There was a long silence. Sander cleared his throat. "Well, I'm just getting set to take the dogs to the park."

"You're going *now*?"

Sander hesitated. "Yes, I thought I would."

"Okay. See you in a few minutes."

Sander looked at the dead phone, then over at Winstead, who was regarding him with a puzzled expression. He shrugged at his dog. "No idea," he said. "Let's load up the twins."

Winstead and Ruby had already incorporated park visits into their bill of rights, and now gazed at Sander expectantly whenever he stood up out of his chair. They tracked him with eager intensity as he fetched their leashes, then bounded joyfully into the minivan, wrestling all the way to the park.

Allison was there, Claire was there, Lucille was there. Sander sat in his vehicle, watching them talk at the picnic table, seriously considering not getting out of the minivan. The twins were kicking expectantly, looking out the windows.

"Well, old boy," Sander murmured to Winstead, "this will be interesting."

# CHAPTER NINETEEN

When he freed the boys, they charged the park playground like Marines hitting a beachhead. Sander watched approvingly as they set about trying to climb the slides from the bottom up instead of using the ladders. The other children seemed a little intimidated by the assault. Sander put the pups in their fenced-off doggie area.

It was a chilly day, this Saturday. Allison was hugging herself and wore a knitted cap. Lucille had on a wool overcoat the same color as her leather boots. Red-headed Claire grinned at him as he approached.

"Ladies," he greeted them awkwardly.

For a long time, that was all he said, but he did gather a lot of what he supposed was good information.

Claire liked sailing in the summer and cross-country skiing in the winter. She was a huge Beatles fan.

Lucille loved to spend time in the kitchen.

Allison claimed to like movies that most women didn't, the kinds with guns and superheroes.

Lucille loved dogs.

Allison said, Oh, I *love* dogs, as if that were somehow a different thing.

"I feel as if I'm on a reality show," Claire said with a laugh.

"Next time we have coffee, let's go to the bookstore," Allison announced viciously. "I just love spending hours with the books."

"So you had coffee," Lucille stated blandly. She looked at Sander with raised eyebrows.

"Well . . ." Sander began, ready to defend himself.

"What a nice . . ." Lucille turned to Claire. "What's the word?"

"Innocent?" Claire suggested.

"*Platonic* thing to do," Lucille decided.

Allison narrowed her eyes to slits.

"They have a nice lunch menu too, Sander, for when you and Allison are ready to take the next big step," Claire informed him with a smile.

"I would love that!" Allison agreed contractually.

"Allie, bless your heart, if you keep losing weight you're just going to up and blow away with the wind," Lucille said, arsenic in the sugar of her voice.

"You didn't even bring your grandchildren with you today," Allison sneered.

"I can't think of a time when I've had a more interesting conversation," Claire observed.

"Whatever happened with Gary?" Allison probed Lucille. "I thought he was going to be your fourth husband for sure."

Sander saw Winstead and Ruby go stock-still in the dog park, as if they sensed a threat. He met their eyes.

"Fourth husband," Lucille repeated with an icy smile.

"So funny, Allie. You know I've only been down the aisle twice."

"And they both died, right?" Allison pressed, her expression positively prosecutorial.

Lucille stood. "This has been so fun, but I need to go. Sander, would you mind walking me to my car? Allison, you'll keep an eye on his boys for a moment, won't you? That's so nice."

Claire gave him a light wave while Allison seethed. Sander escorted Lucille to her Mercedes.

"I was wondering if I could come cook dinner for you sometime. I am a really good cook."

Sander nodded—she'd mentioned her expertise in the kitchen more than once. "I do appreciate the offer," he told her, "but between my granddaughter and me, I think we've got it handled. To tell you the truth, it's been a bit of a bonding experience for both of us. Last night we made enchiladas."

Lucille regarded him intently. "I understand. But I would love to cook for you. And it would seem to me, Sander, that you could use some female company about now."

Sander blinked. Had he heard her correctly?

"That would be nice," he admitted faintly, feeling a little unsteady.

Lucille stepped closer. "Your nanny has the boys on Monday, Wednesday, and Friday, right?"

Sander swallowed dryly. "Yes," he agreed. Was this how women were, now? He had absolutely zero experience with situations like this.

"So, this coming Monday, why don't you come over and I'll make you a nice lunch. With a special dessert."

Sander could think of no reason to say no to this.

"Plan on staying a while, Sander," she suggested. As she said this, she traced her index finger across Sander's jawline, and he shivered.

Ello's skating coach was Mrs. Steigler, a thin woman with hair gone gray, though she couldn't have been much older than thirty. She only took her hands out of her pockets when she was demonstrating something.

Today, as if part of some conspiracy, Mrs. Steigler paired Ello with Mitch for most of the session. They were dancing in closed position, meaning they faced each other. Mitch's right hand felt damp under her shoulder blade as he clutched her a tad too tightly, and at every opportunity he shot her a brooding, intense stare from beneath his preposterously dark eyebrows.

Ello shivered with relief when Mrs. Steigler asked her to demonstrate a toe-step to one of the other girls. Her back felt cool from evaporation where Mitch's hand had been trespassing.

It occurred to Ello that she had ventured out of the emotional dead zone. Her protective shell had slipped. She was back to being irritated with Mitch, back to wanting to quit skating, back to feeling like Things Were Normal—which they weren't, but only if she thought about Mom. And when she thought about Sean . . .

A noise at the far end of the rink drew her eyes. What she saw made her stomach sink. A bunch of girls were loading in for free skate after Ello's lesson. It was obviously some sort of party, with balloons and everything. Maybe someone's birthday. . . .

But they weren't just any girls. It was Brittne and Mourgen and Jayneigh—the ones who, along with a few others, had mutilated the photographs.

"Eloise?" Mrs. Steigler asked. "Do you know those girls?"

Ello turned and gave her skating instructor a flat stare. "No," she responded dully.

Mrs. Steigler glanced at her watch. "Okay," she told everyone, "line up. Let's talk about what we did today."

Ello waited until the class was mostly in a row so that she could skate over and stand next to anyone except Mitch. She saw him struggling to decide whether to break out of formation and join her.

As Mrs. Steigler reviewed the day's progress, Ello spotted a boy in full hockey regalia clomping in front of the bleachers.

He was grinning, of course, because it was Sean.

His awkwardness vanished the moment his blades touched ice. As he flowed out toward them, Mrs. Steigler turned to tell him it wasn't yet free skate, but Ello blurted, "It's okay. He's a good friend," and glided across to meet him. They stopped in the middle of the rink.

Sean shrugged and smiled. "You did all the work," he pointed out. "I just picked you up and set you back down."

They began waltzing, not attempting anything complicated, just moving together. Ello's back faced the direction they were skating, which meant trusting Sean, whose hand was precisely where Mitch's had been. Sean's touch was light, featherlight, and Ello felt it as a tingle. They talked and skated, smiling, their rotation taking them past the party to which Ello had not been invited. She never looked once.

Later, Ello positively bounced into her car seat, throwing her bag at her feet. She grinned at Sander, who grinned back at her.

"Good lesson today?"

"Yes!"

Ewan said something and Sander shook his head. "Did you just ask for a donut?" he chided. "We do not stop for donuts."

"You understood that?" Ello asked suspiciously.

Sander shrugged. "I may have picked up a little Twinglish here and there, though mostly I can't understand a word they're saying."

"A donut does sound pretty good," Ello admitted.

"So, you're seconding the motion?" Sander asked slyly.

Ello frowned. "What?"

"Never mind."

After a moment, Ello sighed. "Grandpa?"

"Yeah?"

"At my ice dancing? I did denial. I've been doing it all day."

Sander nodded. "Yeah, me too, Ello."

Sander panfried some walleye and Ello prepared a peppery cream cheese shrimp sauce to put on top. He simmered carrots and broccoli in butter and chicken broth, and Ello made a salad. The boys chomped on the carrots and ate a frozen cheese pizza that Ello baked for them.

Hunter, of course, was at the hospital, but they set a place for him anyway. Sander focused on cutting pizza into pieces and trying to catch the ones the twins threw. Sometimes the dogs beat him to it.

Sander watched Ello, worried about her uncharacteristic silence, but she seemed to be in a happy place, so he didn't try to draw her out.

The Christmas tree was unwrapped and in its stand in front of the window. It remained a tight column of pine boughs, stubbornly maintaining its bound-up shape.

"Maybe it will loosen up during the night," Sander observed.

Ello helped him bathe the boys and shove them into their beds. Sander read them a story about a dog, a rabbit, and a hawk, all of whom became great friends despite the fact that two of them probably wanted to eat the other.

It had been a day. He climbed into bed with a weary groan. As he drifted off, a phrase kept turning up in his thoughts.

*Female company.*

He was pretty sure that meant exactly what it sounded like. Somehow he had gone from having no company of the female kind to having three separate widows seemingly try to outbid each other for his attention. How was that possible? Alley Allison seemed almost desperate. Red-headed Claire blazed him with her clear eyes, and seemed to be reading him like a blueprint. And Lucille, with her talk of cooking and . . . other stuff . . . was taking aim at his, well, his appetites.

Had this really all happened in such a short period of time?

Sleep was deep and dreamless. And then he started awake. Ello was standing next to his bed, peering down at him. It was past three in the morning.

"Are you okay?" he whispered. Her expression was too shadowed for him to read it.

"Grandpa? Can you come see something?"

# CHAPTER TWENTY

Sander followed Ello down the tenebrous hallway, his feet dry on the wood floor. They were padding as silently as they could, though the twins probably could have slept through an artillery barrage.

"Ello?" he murmured as they entered the living room. The absurd thought struck Sander that she might be sleep-walking.

"Wait right there," she urged. The curtains were drawn, the room dark, the couch aglow from some ambient illumination from the kitchen. He frowned as she went to her knees and fumbled with something he couldn't see.

And then he gasped with surprise. She had carefully strung the multicolored Christmas lights around the tree; when she lit them, they set the whole room ablaze.

Ello's face was as bright as the lights. "See?" she whispered triumphantly. "It's a perfect tree!"

He looked closer and saw that she was right; the branches had surrendered to gravity and resumed their normal relationship with one another, rendering the tree as symmetrical as any Sander had ever seen.

Ello was literally bouncing up and down with glee, and

"I've heard there are other locales you can go to in the winter," Claire remarked. "There's no law that you have to stay here. They don't detain you at the border or anything."

Sander laughed but couldn't come up with a clever rejoinder.

They had reached their cars. It suddenly seemed wrong that they were about to drive away from each other. "Claire . . ."

She regarded him with one eyebrow raised, her brown eyes friendly.

"Why don't we have lunch. My treat, of course. Unless you're . . ." He gestured to the whole rest of the world, because she could have had anything planned.

She shook her head. "Nope, I'm not going anywhere or doing anything. Lunch sounds like fun."

They picked a place on Front Street to meet and eat. As he followed her, Sander looked in the rearview mirror, where Winstead would be if he had come along for the ride. "Do you think this is a coincidence?" he asked his absent dog.

Hunter met Dr. Lombard at her request in her office, which had a couch and a few chairs in what he felt was an oddly incongruent fashion, making the space feel like a psychiatrist's lair, built for conversation. Perhaps it had to do with her specialty, "intensivist," a field of medicine Hunter had never heard of before.

Dr. Lombard was a slim and elegant woman with an accent Hunter had originally misidentified as British, but which turned out to be South African. She had striking eyes, but Hunter felt sure he saw a grim purpose in them now.

"Thank you so much for coming to see me," Dr. Lombard said.

Hunter nodded and swallowed, bracing himself.

"I want to speak to you about Juliana's condition. How do you think she's doing?"

Hunter was surprised. Why did it matter what *he* thought?

Dr. Lombard seemed to read his mind. "I ask because you've been here virtually around the clock. No one else has been observing Juliana so intently."

"I don't see much of a change at all," Hunter confessed.

Dr. Lombard nodded. "Precisely. I want you to know that I am a bit baffled as to why she is in this static state. Normally—almost always, in fact—a patient would show signs of recovery by now, or else . . ." Her eyes turned sympathetic, and Hunter could have finished the statement for her. When she saw that he understood, she continued. "We have her on dialysis, which is one of my main concerns—her kidneys. And we've been doing daily blood draws, and"—she glanced down at some papers on the table between them—"I'm concerned about some of her numbers. They aren't improving."

Hunter licked dry lips. "Dr. Lombard?"

"Yes?"

"Are you telling me my wife is going to die?"

❆

"I worked for the Saturn division of GM in Detroit until 2009," Sander told Claire autobiographically. "Basically, my job was to try to prevent the spread of GM's lethargy to what was supposed to be a new, innovative brand. Did pretty well until the UAW dissolved their labor pact and treated us the same as every other division. That pretty much ended it. So I decided, what the heck, I always liked building things, and went to work putting up houses for a contractor."

Claire raised her eyebrows at that. "You started building houses. In Detroit. In 2009," she summarized slowly.

Sander laughed. "Oh, I know. For a while there it looked like I was the only rat swimming to the sinking ship. But even though the market tanked, there were still people who wanted to build their own places and could afford to hire us. We had a good reputation."

"I would love to give you a list of things that are going wrong in my house," Claire observed wryly.

"I'd be happy to help."

"Oh, no," she replied, shaking her head. "I wouldn't do that, have you over to my place for home repair."

"Oh." He frowned.

"You were thinking you would come to my house and

rescue me from my appliances," she teased. "The hero with a toolbelt."

"Something like that," he admitted. He smiled at how easily she had read him.

"Sometimes I think the choices we make early on can have an effect on how things turn out later," Claire advised. It sounded like a lighthearted observation, but when she peered at him, it was as if they were speaking about something else entirely. She did that a lot, it seemed.

Hunter felt a presence in his bedroom doorway and turned.

"Welcome back," Sander greeted him.

Hunter shrugged. "Just thought I should maybe put on some fresh clothes."

"Any change?"

Hunter shook his head. "No. Everything okay here?"

"Ello and I got it all handled."

Hunter grunted and looked around. "Okay, I just had my car keys in my hand. Where the heck did I put them?"

"Speaking of that," Sander said after a moment, "I'm thinking of selling the Monte Carlo."

Hunter looked up sharply. "*What?*"

"Yeah."

"But that thing's your pride and joy, Dad. You clean it with a toothbrush."

"It's just a car, Hunter," Sander replied levelly. "Yet even without its engine, you're right; it's in pristine condition.

But I'd like to park something else in its place in the garage. Something fun. Sort of tired of driving around in a minivan."

Hunter grinned. It felt strange, stretching his face, an expression long disused. "What? You don't feel masculine cruising around with pony stickers in your window?"

Later that day, Hunter stepped out of Juliana's hospital room and checked his text messages. The only work-related item was from Kim, complaining that when people opened the front door, cold air came in.

He suspected he knew why Mrs. O'Brien hadn't reached out. He'd done the same thing himself—frozen out an employee he knew was about to be terminated. She probably saw no point in wasting further words on Hunter Goss.

Still, he hadn't been fired. Yet.

He dialed Robert Gethers, the CFO of Colfaxette. Prepared for voicemail, Hunter started in surprise when Robert answered.

They agreed that the winter was oddly dry. They decided the Detroit Lions wouldn't make the playoffs next year, either. Their chitchat was as artful as Ello ice dancing with a partner, each skating around and around in synchronous avoidance of the topic at hand.

*Well, time to face the music.* "So, hey, Robert, about the furniture . . . I guess there was some damage." Hunter laughed dryly as if there was something funny in all this.

And maybe characterizing the complete destruction of the shelves as "some damage" *was* funny. Hilarious, even.

"Yeah, I saw the scratch on that one desk. It's not too bad, and it's sort of an extra one anyway. No problem," came the reply.

Hunter paused, pondering his answer. "Well, sure, but the hutches sort of broke apart. . . . I'm sure you noticed."

Robert said, "Oh, yeah, that."

*Yeah, that.*

"It actually sort of saved us some effort, since nobody wanted the hutches anyway. Our offices already have built-in shelving. We were just going to throw the things out."

Hunter gripped the phone. "So everything's okay?"

Robert sighed. "No, not okay. That's why I've been dodging your calls. Our next round of funding is held up, and I'm running on fumes here. I can't process your invoice for payment until probably after the first of the year. I'm sorry— I made the agreement in good faith—but you know how it is."

Hunter considered this. He had gone from *Tell them we're not going to pay to have the junk removed* to *I'll have to wait for payment until after the first of the year.*

"I understand. That's fine, Robert."

"It is? Oh, man, I owe you one."

"No problem," Hunter answered faintly.

This minor reprieve wouldn't salvage his career, but it was something.

❉

Ruby greeted Hunter when he walked in the door, going crazy with joy. He tossed his keys down and patted his pockets for his cell phone. He returned to the car to retrieve it, and when he walked back in Ruby was waiting, wagging and licking, so happy to see him again that Hunter fell to his knees and put his hands out for the little dog. "You silly . . . you just saw me ten seconds ago. Oh, Ruby, Ruby, Ruby," Hunter murmured to the wiggling puppy. "You're not going anywhere, are you, little dog? Even if Ello could give you up, I can't. You can live with me and my family in the homeless shelter." He peered into the canine's innocent eyes. "I've made a mess of my career, Ruby. Things are going to be pretty bad soon. And if Juliana doesn't recover, that will truly be the end of me, baby girl," he whispered.

When Hunter released her, Ruby darted off with crazed energy, racing around the room in celebration, because puppies know how to celebrate everything.

Hunter meandered into the kitchen to see what his father and daughter were making for dinner. He jerked in surprise: an attractive older woman was bustling around, and wonderful cooking odors were coming from something sizzling on the stovetop. She turned and grinned at him. "Hi!" she greeted him. "You must be Hunter."

# CHAPTER TWENTY-ONE

To Hunter's utter shock, the woman tossed off her oven mitts like a hockey player getting ready to fight, but instead of taking a swing at him she moved across the kitchen and gathered him in a forceful hug. Hunter was immediately uncomfortable with how much chest was pushing into his.

"You poor man," she whispered. "Sander told me about your wife. Is she doing any better?"

"No." He extricated himself from her soft embrace. "But she's not any worse, either. That's all we can cling to at the moment, but . . . I'm sorry, who are you again?"

She laughed. "I am a friend of your father's."

"My father?" Hunter repeated, as if he had never met the man.

"A very special friend," she corrected herself. "He's out in the backyard playing with his grandkids. I'm Lucille."

Now they shook hands, though after the hug it seemed like a weak second act. Hunter looked away from the teardrop opening below her neckline. Then he walked over to the sliding doors and joined Winstead. The backyard spotlights were stabbing out into the darkness, and the light flurry of snow that had been filling the air with desultory flakes seemed to be gathering a bit more energy, producing white flares in the harsh beams. Winstead was watching anxiously as Sander, the twins, and Ello endeavored to place the middle portion of a snowman on top of the big round base that had already been positioned. Ruby hadn't joined Hunter and Winstead; instead, she was industriously shredding a rope toy in a corner of the dining room.

"What do you think, Winstead?" Hunter asked. "Dad just seems really different all of a sudden."

Winstead glanced up at him, then returned to sentry duty. Hunter turned back to the kitchen, trying to think of something else to say to Lucille, gave up, and went down the hall to change into jeans. In his bedroom, he knocked at the back window, and Sander and Ello stood and waved cheerfully. Ewan celebrated his father's arrival by throwing a fistful of snow into Garrett's face.

When they all came charging back inside the house to change out of their wet clothes, Hunter took his father aside.

"So, Dad, who's this Lucille?"

"Oh," Sander answered. "She's one of the women I'm seeing."

"What?" Hunter stared incredulously.

"She's a widow," Sander added, as if that explained everything. "How's your wife?"

"No change. I just got tired of commissary food."

"Well, you picked the right night to come home for dinner. Lucille sure knows her way around a kitchen."

Lucille had made something out of a delicate white wine sauce and chicken and other unidentifiable but delicious-smelling ingredients. She wouldn't eat with them, though. She insisted that the family enjoy their privacy, especially considering that their mother was still in the hospital. "I can't wait to meet her," Lucille added. Ello frowned suspiciously. Winstead sighed. Ruby licked the woman's pants.

"I'll walk you to your car," Sander offered.

Lucille waved a cheerful goodbye and left with Sander, her arm through his and her head briefly touching his shoulder.

The second she was gone, Ello whirled on Hunter. "Who *is* that? Is that, like, Grandpa's *girlfriend*?"

"It's one of the women he's been seeing," Hunter advised blandly.

Ello flinched as if he'd just sprayed her with a fire hose.

They delayed for a few moments, then decided that the food smelled too good to wait for Sander to get back. His absence from the table, as it became more and more prolonged, built up an awkwardness for Ello and her father to share. She broke the silence first. "What could he be doing for this long?"

"Well . . ." Hunter began slowly, "they are dating each other. I suppose that he's, um, saying goodnight."

Ello's eyes bulged. "You mean they're making out?" she shrieked. "That's gross! He's so old!"

Hunter couldn't help but laugh at her.

"God, this is the weirdest family on earth," Ello lamented.

When he finally stopped laughing, Hunter leaned forward tenderly. "Ello, I just want to tell you how much I appreciate all that you've done. I know that between my work and being at the hospital, I haven't been around at all. And you and your grandfather have picked up the slack and done everything. I am so proud of you."

Ello's eyes were shining. Ruby, sensing something, left her station under Ewan's chair, sidled over to Ello, and stared up at her.

That reminded Hunter. "So, are you making any progress finding a home for Ruby?" he asked lightly.

Ello shook her head, guilty as a thief lit up by spotlights.

"Well, I guess Mom's going to be pretty surprised to find out we have a new puppy."

Ello stared at him as the full impact of what he was saying landed on her. When she rushed over and wrapped him in a little-girl hug, Hunter felt all the stresses of the day fall away.

After dinner, Sander suggested that he and Hunter go for a walk with the dogs. Winstead seemed to be in favor of this suggestion, and Ruby was excited because Winstead was excited. Hunter demurred, saying he really needed to get back to the hospital.

Sander shook his head. "I know Juliana. She would want you to spend some time with your family."

Hunter thought about it and nodded. "Well, but the boys

are in bed, and Ello is in her room staring at her phone with her headphones on. So I think I'm good."

"Sure," Sander drawled, "but I'm family, too, you know."

It was a good point. They struggled into boots, coats, gloves, and hats, leashed up the dogs, and clomped out into the snow. It was a quiet night, the crunch of their footsteps and the gentle sawing of their breathing almost all that they could hear. They walked in silence, stopping every few feet so that Winstead could mark his territory.

"So, this Lucille . . ." Hunter began. "Is it serious?"

"Oh, no, the thing with Lucille is not serious. But it is *fun*," Sander responded dryly.

"She seems really nice. She's a great cook. And she's a bit of a babe, Dad," Hunter confided.

Sander grinned. "Yes, she is. But she's also a little pushy. She's already talking about how we should move in together, even sort of made it sound like a done deal. She lives out at Potter Road and Three Mile, south of town. I'm not ready for anything like that yet."

"Wow. I had no idea."

"A lot's been happening while you've been away."

"You said *one* of the women you're seeing," Hunter prodded shrewdly.

"Well, I went out with a widow named Allison. But she's very clingy, very needy. It's like whatever I do disappoints her. The whole *world* seems to disappoint her. We were having coffee, and they didn't have any of that sugar that comes in a brown bag, just the white stuff. Which, once you put it in coffee, tastes the exact same, but it ruined her whole day. You know what I mean?"

"Honestly, no," Hunter confessed. "Any other widows?"

Sander chuckled softly. "Well, there's this woman named Claire. She and I get along pretty well. It's just friends right now, though."

They crunched on in comfortable silence. Sander glanced at his son. "How does it feel? I mean, me seeing other women—women other than your mother, I mean."

Hunter considered it. "How does it feel? I'm not sure I feel anything, Dad. I still think about Mom every single day. But most of all, I want you to be happy. It seems like you haven't been happy for a long, long time."

Sander sighed. "I know. When your mom died, happiness seemed impossible—so I've been trying to settle for just not feeling awful. But you know what? I think maybe, now, I've got a shot at it. Happiness, I'm saying. But not because of these . . . widows. It's because I have a reason for me to get out of bed in the morning. I have a function in this world. I matter to people. I matter to Ello, I matter to the twins."

"You matter to me, Dad," Hunter said softly. The two men stopped and faced each other and, for a moment, it seemed like they might hug.

The mood passed. Hunter kicked at a chunk of ice, sending it skittering. Winstead stared at it alertly as it shot past, but didn't strain at the leash.

"So," Hunter began, his tone indicating a change of

subject. "They're letting me go January second. My company, I mean."

Sander and Hunter both looked equally shocked at this pronouncement. Hunter hadn't articulated it out loud to anyone, not even himself, until this moment.

"Why?" Sander demanded, aghast.

Hunter explained how the engineers had sabotaged his innovations with cardboard barriers. Many had eyeholes cut in them so people could stare out with baleful eyeballs, like portraits in a haunted house.

Sander was outraged. "They're going to fire you for *that*? You should just tell them to take down the boxes. It's a fire hazard!"

Hunter grinned wryly. "Sadly, it doesn't work like that. These guys have skills that are in high demand; they can work anywhere. We have enough problems with attrition as it is. I give them an ultimatum, they'll just leave. Recruitment is one of our biggest soft costs."

"You should show them video of an office fire. That'd change a few minds."

"That's right. . . . I forgot you were with the fire department."

"Loved that job. Your mom made me quit, though. Afraid I was going to burn up."

"When I was a boy I used to climb the dresser and open your drawer to look at your badge in the leather wallet," Hunter confessed.

Sander nodded. "Still got that thing, actually. I should probably think of a better place to hide it; won't be long before the twins are invading my drawers. They'd love taking the badge to school and telling their friends they're firemen."

Hunter suddenly stopped under a streetlight. Sander peered at him in the odd, desaturating glare. "What is it, son?"

There were only ten days left until Christmas. Sander had noticed that, whereas the twins were taking in the decorations and presents and tree like triple shots of espresso, a dark weariness had settled over Ello, each day without her mother sapping her vitality.

On the way to school, Ello's phone buzzed at her. "It's Dad, doing Skype." She answered. "Hi, Dad."

Sander felt himself take in a breath and hold it. This was what he dreaded most: a call from his son at the hospital.

"Can you guys pull over for a minute?" Hunter requested.

Ello turned to her grandfather with a gaze full of fear and pleading. Sander couldn't think of anything to say to help. He flashed back to how he felt when his wife exhaled her last breath, how the desperation broke over him and he wanted just one more moment, just one more second, but she was gone.

His heart thudding, Sander steered over to the curb. The boys, in back, remained oblivious. Sander put the van in park and Ello angled her phone so they both could be on the call. Their father's face filled the screen. "There's something I want you to see," Hunter told them.

The image on the phone bounced and then settled on Juliana. She was still hooked up to all the tubes and all the wires.

But her eyes were open.

# CHAPTER TWENTY-TWO

J uliana's throat hurt from the back of her tongue all the way down into her lungs. She could not remember ever feeling anything so awful as trying to swallow past her tortured tracheal passage.

And she really couldn't. Swallow, that was, because it seemed all her muscles were paralyzed. Was this what had happened to her? Was she a quadriplegic? She could move her eyes and she did so, taking in her husband as he sat at her bedside. He was crying, which led Juliana to conclude her fears were exactly right. Something horrible had happened, and she'd never walk again. *Car accident?* Had she severed her spine in a wreck so horrible she couldn't remember it?

*What happened to me?*

After a moment's thought, that didn't seem right. Aside from the pain in her throat, she could feel an ache in her back and cramps in her calves. *That's good, right? That I can still experience pain?*

Okay, she couldn't move, but she had feeling in her limbs, which maybe meant she could recover from this after all.

Because she had to recover. The twins needed her. The whole house would collapse into chaos. *Help,* she wanted to scream. *Help me.*

A short, heavy, Hispanic man stood behind Hunter, wearing a white coat like a doctor on television. He even carried a clipboard, although the wardrobe department had failed to supply him with a stethoscope. He was looking down at her with a benign, tolerant expression. Juliana had never seen him before, and he didn't bother introducing himself.

"Hi, honey. How do you feel?" Hunter asked.

Juliana couldn't reply. She decided against blinking an answer, because that seemed ridiculous. *I should be able to talk!* Even paralyzed people could talk.

"You can't talk," the doctor advised her. "But the fact that you can breathe on your own already is a really beautiful sign."

Juliana pondered his use of the word "beautiful."

"You're really weak," Hunter informed her.

Juliana wished they would stop mansplaining what she could discern perfectly well on her own! Hunter was patting her hand, and she could feel that, too.

"You had pyelonephritis, which put you in renal failure," the doctor continued dispassionately. "After your seizure, we put you in a coma."

She'd had a *seizure*?

"Unfortunately, you're currently experiencing the results of critical illness myopathy," he told her.

Juliana looked to Hunter.

"You can't move your muscles," her husband elaborated. "But you're going to get better, honey."

"Well," the doctor said, "I'll let the two of you talk."

Apparently only Juliana saw the irony in his statement. *I can't talk*. In fact, she couldn't even move her tongue.

Hunter leaned down, his face full of concern. "I know this must be confusing," he told her. "So, what happened was, you were sick. Do you remember that?" He watched her until it seemed to register that she could not nod. So he did it for her. "Right, so you were sick, and then it seemed like you were better, even though you were pretty weak. And then you got really bad. You were completely unresponsive, so we had an ambulance bring you here. Then you were in a coma for eleven days."

Had she been able, Juliana would have widened her eyes in shock. Eleven *days*?

"It's affecting all your muscles. That's why you can't move much."

Juliana processed this.

"The doctors say that's not unheard of, even though I never heard of it before. So now what's going to happen is, you're going to gradually get stronger. Soon you'll be able to chew food and move your arms and all that. Meanwhile, you're on daily dialysis. They've got you on an IV, but they say as early as tomorrow or the next day I'll be able to feed you liquids." Hunter leaned even closer. "I'll be here for you, darling. I'll take care of you."

Tears began flowing from her unblinking eyes. Hunter grabbed a tissue and dabbed them away.

"Hey," he said hoarsely. "I really thought I was going to lose you, Juliana. We all did."

The first helping of thin chicken broth Hunter spooned into Juliana's mouth a few days later burned her throat. It felt wonderful. She'd never considered that food could be more than just taste; it was an all-body sensation, igniting every cell.

Juliana could tell she'd lost considerable weight. She wondered if she should write a weight-loss book: *How to Lose Twenty Pounds, in a Coma.*

She was still largely helpless. She couldn't talk; for some reason, the words just didn't form into sounds that could crawl out. Instead, they were getting stuck somewhere between her brain and her mouth. But the doctor told her that now that she was swallowing, speech could come at any moment.

Hunter was taking the physical therapist's instructions seriously and had spent many hours massaging her hands and arms. He would lift one leg, put it down, lift the other, put it down, over and over and over. Juliana watched him in wonder. This was the man she'd thought wouldn't lift a finger to help her? Now, when lifting a finger was literally something she could not accomplish on her own, he was doing it all.

"Hunter," she rasped.

They both looked startled that she had said something.

He grinned delightedly. "See? Just like the doctor said. You'll be back to making lists and talking to yourself in no time."

Was that how he saw her? The list-master general?

"Hunter," she repeated in the barest of whispers. "Hunter."

Moments later, her eyes flicked once and shut. Hunter shuddered, because that brought it all back: the persistent conviction that he was losing her forever. Then the gratitude flowed through him like a drug. He was *not* losing her. He let himself believe it, feel it. The woman he loved was not going to die.

Hunter watched his sleeping wife for a long time.

Would it be considered lying to his spouse, he wondered, if he failed to mention that he'd be out of a job after the first of the year?

When Juliana opened her eyes, Ello was looking down at her. She felt her heart skip at the sight of her daughter, who cleared the wet from her cheeks with a battered tissue.

"Mom," Ello whispered. "Oh my God, I was so scared. I just . . ."

More than anything, Juliana wanted to reach out and hug her daughter, assure her she was fine, but her arms still refused to respond to the signals from her brain, her muscles absolutely slack and worthless. "Ello, it's okay. I'm going to be fine. I get better every day. Come hug me," she slurred.

Ello crawled onto the bed like a little girl, wrapped her arms around her mother, pushed her face into Juliana's chest, and began sobbing. Juliana closed her eyes. "It's okay," she repeated, knowing it was the truth because it simply had to be.

Ello had recovered and moved off the bed by the time Sander strolled in. Juliana stared in shock: the man's hair was cut, his face was shaved, there was a color besides parchment-white to his cheeks, and he was wearing a nice sweater.

How long had she *really* been unconscious?

"You had us really worried, honey," Sander told her. He bent down and kissed her forehead, and she caught a whiff of the aftershave he'd worn back when his wife was alive. Juliana turned a bewildered stare at her daughter, who simply shrugged.

"Grandpa and I run the house now," Ello explained. "Dad still has some sort of huge crisis at work, and so we have to do everything."

"Don't worry, the twins are still alive." Sander chuckled. "They tell me we can bring them in to visit you once you're out of ICU and able to defend yourself against their onslaught."

"We cook and everything," Ello boasted.

Sander nodded. "Last night we had chicken lasagna. Pretty good. It was Ello's idea. The twins had hamburgers.

They gave most of them to the dogs." Ello's eyes widened and she stared in alarm at her grandfather.

But Juliana didn't catch the plural—"dogs." She was picturing being in her kitchen, her sons eating hamburger pieces, and it made her so homesick she felt ready to cry. She held it together, though, until Sander and Ello waved goodbye. Then the tears flowed, pooling up and sliding down her face because she couldn't wipe them away.

Sander accepted Lucille's invitation to dinner without realizing that she was taking him to a restaurant. His imagination had led him to picture them dining in her large home—a candlelit meal, perhaps. She was an excellent cook, of course, but there might have been other reasons he was looking forward to being alone with her in her house. His visits there thus far had been—well, successful.

A woman asking a man out to a restaurant was a fairly new experience for him, but Sander was evolving. That's what he told himself, anyway.

On his way back from the men's room, their salad course having just been cleared from the table, Sander saw Lucille on her cell phone. He pulled up short. What was the etiquette in this situation, he wondered?

Lucille had worn her blond hair high off her neck, like a woman going to the Oscars or something. Her black wool skirt looked good with her boots, and he liked the way her white sweater fit her under the short jacket. Her overcoat had been a long cashmere item, the fourth expensive-looking coat he recalled her wearing. Lucille, he reflected ruefully, was a woman of sophisticated but costly tastes.

She caught sight of him out of the corner of her eye and waved him over, so he weaved around the small tables and slid down into his chair.

"I'm just saying, dear, that there's nothing wrong with making a man feel appreciated," Lucille explained into the phone. She gave Sander a wink, which baffled him. "It's not a 'tactic,' as you say." She pulled the phone slightly away and mouthed, "Allison."

Sander wondered if Allison called Lucille as often as she called him.

"I am so sorry you feel that way, but as far as I am concerned, we can all be friends. Nothing has changed," Lucille soothed. "Do you want to talk to him?"

Sander started shaking his head, then twitched in surprise when Lucille extended the telephone to him and he saw that it was his. He locked eyes with Lucille for a moment and her expression turned mischievous.

"I saw who was calling," she whispered with a shrug.

"Hello?" Sander greeted cautiously.

"Sorry to interrupt your date," Allison grumbled.

"Oh. Well . . ." Sander replied inadequately.

"I suppose there's nothing for us to talk about."

Sander agreed with this statement so absolutely, he didn't reply.

"I cut my hair yesterday, but now you'll never see it," Allison griped. "You really led me on, Sander."

Had he? Sander was bewildered. How did listening to complaints constitute leading a woman on?

"Have fun. With *Lucille,*" Allison sneered, breaking the connection. Sander held the phone out, gazing at it in wonder, then looked to Lucille.

"That girl wouldn't know happiness if it got down on one knee and proposed marriage," Lucille observed wryly. "So, Sander . . . I made us dinner reservations for February fourteenth."

Sander blinked at her. "February?"

Lucille threw back her head and laughed. "My, it *has* been a long time for you, hasn't it?"

"A long time . . ." Sander repeated dumbly.

"Sander. February fourteenth is Valentine's Day. Surely you've heard of it."

"Yes, right, of course."

"My favorite restaurant. Bobby's Beef and Crab."

"Don't believe I've ever eaten there."

Lucille leaned forward, her eyes meeting his. "That's because it's in Florida. I made us reservations because I want you to come stay with me at my place in Fort Myers. It's right on the beach." She sat back, a satisfied smile on her face. "Do you think we should have another glass of wine?"

Ello was sitting on her bed, with Ruby sprawled, exhausted, at her feet. Periodically she moved her toes along the puppy's back. She was texting with some friends from outside

Brittne's orbit, listening to music, and idly reflecting on the fact that she had taken care of Garrett and Ewan, shoving dinner at them and cramming them into bed, and it had all been *fine*. The screaming resentment she'd always felt when asked to watch her brothers, back when Life Had Been Perfect Before They Were Born, hadn't made an appearance. Sander was on a date, Dad was late coming home from the hospital, Mom was still sick, and Ello Was Handling It, an important and productive member of the family. It made Brittne and Mourgen and their crowd seem like *children*.

Suddenly, a text from Sean O'Brien flashed on her screen.

SOB: Can you talk? URGENT!

# CHAPTER TWENTY-THREE

Ello anxiously waited for Sean's call, not sure what to expect. What did it mean that it was *urgent*? She reached down to stroke Ruby. "Maybe he has to move back to Detroit," she fretted. "Or maybe he's got a girlfriend."

*Brittne.*

Ello sucked in a breath. If Brittne decided she wanted him, then Sean would be Brittne's.

Why wasn't he calling? It was "urgent," and He Was Taking Forever.

Ruby lifted her head and looked at Ello, clearly picking up on her distress.

Finally, her phone rang.

"Hi!" Sean greeted her cheerfully, as if he hadn't pre-burdened the call.

"Hey," Ello replied cautiously.

"How's everything?"

OMG. Ello wondered if Sean had ever had a bad day or dark thought in his entire dimpled life. "Okay. My mom's getting better every day. They're hopefully going to send her home soon."

"That's great!"

Ello's heart was still pounding. "So, what's up?"

"Oh. So I mentioned to my mom that I'd like to have you come over after school for a study date. Like, I'm finishing up your biography, and I have a few questions."

Ello gripped the phone more tightly. *Study date?* He hadn't mentioned this to her.

"Oh?"

"Right. And she went rage mode."

Ello was still processing "study date." She pictured the two of them sitting side by side on the couch, the music on, a fire in the fireplace. . . . She frowned. "Rage mode? What do you mean? Why?"

"Exactly." Sean lowered his voice. "So, you know your dad works for my mom? She's like the CEO of the company."

"Right. But his job is important too, I mean, he runs all the departments in the building," Ello responded defensively, if inaccurately.

Sean was silent.

"What is it, Sean?"

"Just, my mom said that a relationship between us would be very awkward for her. Like it's any of her business, right?"

Ello held her breath. A Relationship Between Us? Then she shook her head wildly. "Are you saying your mom told you we can't be friends?" she demanded, her voice a lamentable squeak.

Sean went quiet again.

"Sean?"

"Look, I'm not supposed to tell you this, but my mom said that after the first of the year, your dad's going to be fired."

Ello gasped.

"I'm really sorry," Sean babbled in a rush, "but I thought I should tell you. Like, if your dad gets weird, or maybe needs your support."

"Okay," Ello agreed numbly. *Fired.*

"Are you all right?"

"Yes. Sure."

"Should I have told you? I shouldn't have said anything. I'm sorry."

"No, Sean," she assured him faintly. "I'm glad you did."

They said goodbye. Ello curled up on her bed, clutching her stomach as if crumpled over from a biting cramp. Ruby roused herself and licked her face.

Ello had an awful, awful secret. There were other implications to her call with Sean, but this was all she could focus on. She buried her face in Ruby's fur for a moment, then suddenly pulled back. "Oh my God . . ." she breathed.

No wonder her parents seemed so strained with each other. No wonder they were talking about getting divorced. Ello felt a flash of pure fury at her mother. Dad needed help and support and Mom said she'd leave him if he didn't make enough *money*? *That's* the kind of person she was?

Except . . . that *wasn't* the kind of person her mom was. Ello shook her head, the anger draining out. Juliana cared a lot, about a whole lot of things—whole *lists* of things—but Mom wasn't what you would call a material girl.

Ello's eyes widened as another thought occurred.

*What if Dad doesn't know?*

Sander sat comfortably under the gray Michigan sky, Claire on the bench next to him. They were watching her grandchildren and the twins play a complicated game that was mostly about falling backward in the snow as if shot by a sniper.

"The older one is Calvin," Sander observed.

"That he is," Claire agreed.

Sander smiled. "Just pointing out how good I'm getting at remembering things I never thought were important. He's six. He's got your hair."

"My hair?"

"Thick and dark, I mean. But you've got some red in yours, I think. Like, auburn."

"I've got some red I've *put* in mine, you mean." Claire laughed.

Sander plunged on determinedly. "Jenner's younger than the twins, and he's got *my* hair." Sander pointed to his white, thin wisps.

"Your expression looks as if you are complimenting me, Sander, but I am having trouble finding the flattery in your words."

Sander laughed.

His phone vibrated. He reflexively pulled it out and sighed.

"Everything okay?" Claire asked.

He shook his head. "It's Allison. She wants to get together to work things out between us. And I texted back, 'What things?'"

"Ah. So you text with Allison, and Lucille says you took her out to dinner two nights ago," Claire observed with a glint in her clear eyes.

Sander had to prevent himself from wincing. "Well, to be entirely accurate, Lucille took me out to dinner."

Claire regarded him with an odd smile. "You're quite the popular one, aren't you? There aren't really any eligible men your age around here, you know. And by 'eligible' I mean normal, non-neurotic, kind, handsome. And then suddenly you burst onto the scene."

Sander wondered what "scene" she was talking about. The singles scene? The dating scene? "Until recently, I didn't get out much," he admitted. "As in, ever. Didn't have much of a reason to, really. Then my daughter-in-law got sick and we all had to pitch in." He gestured to the twins, who had abandoned the other children and were playing a game where they sprawled lengthwise across the swings and then tried to move back and forth to ram the crowns of their heads together. "It's not bad, kid duty."

A long, comfortable pause followed. Sander couldn't put a word to what he was feeling. . . . Was there such a thing as excited contentment?

"I'm hearing now that when a man wants to kiss a

woman, he's got to ask permission," he speculated idly, the thought coming out of nowhere.

This broadened her smile. "You say it like that's a bad thing," she noted. "But is it, really? I think it's fine that a man tests the waters, don't you?"

"Just sort of seems to take the fun out of it a little," Sander grunted.

Claire arched her eyebrows. "Oh, I promise you, if it gets to that, we will have *fun*."

Sander's heart beat faster as they gazed at each other; then Claire's expression turned serious. "You know, I was never a beauty contestant."

Sander frowned. "I think you're beautiful," he told her before he could consider the wisdom of such a statement. Because she *was*. It wasn't just her clear complexion and re-markable eyes; there was a delightful exuberance he found damned appealing. Lucille impressed him too, but her perfect makeup and perfect hair and expensive clothing always felt a bit too much like packaging, somehow. And Allison had smiled once or twice and looked cute when she did so, but it was an expression she rarely deployed.

"Why, thank you, Mr. Goss. But what I meant was, I never participated in one of those things where the women line up and compete for the crown against each other."

"I see," Sander replied, even though he didn't.

"I've just noticed that, as far as Lucille and Allison are concerned, there's some sort of competition going on. And I'm telling you, I'm not good at that sort of thing."

The whole situation was so ludicrous as to make Sander

smile. He tried to picture how it could possibly be true that there were multiple women *competing* for him. *Come on. I'm no ladies' man.*

Claire cocked her head at him. "Do you understand what I'm saying, here? I'm not interested in trying to out-woman the other women."

"Oh." What she was saying made perfect sense. Oddly, Sander's first feeling was one of disappointment.

"That doesn't mean I don't enjoy your company," she assured him, reaching out and touching his arm.

"I like being with you too."

"Let's just leave things like that, then. Until you get tired of playing the field, that is."

That seemed significant. She nodded at the question implicit in his expression. "Oh, I'm saying I'm interested, Sander. Very. You're kind to your grandchildren. You have a good sense of humor—meaning, you laugh at my jokes." She grinned. "I find it easy and free being with you."

Their eyes locked, and Sander felt the floor of his stomach drop out. He was the first to look away. "Guess I didn't think about it that way—playing the field," he confessed. "It was more that I went to the park, and the next thing I knew . . ." He shrugged.

The kids were getting tired; Sander could tell by the way Ewan was kicking at the snow, trying to spray his brother with it as they pendulumed back and forth on the swings. There was a lethargy to his actions, like suddenly he was only going through the motions of being a rampaging toddler.

"It was about two years after my Bill died. My husband. Two years before I felt as if I were back in control of my life— that instead of things happening *to* me, pushing me around like a bully, I could make my own choices." Claire patted his arm. "Forgive me for saying so, but I think you're where I was: past the two-year mark. You can seize control of your destiny. It just depends what you want."

Sander nodded.

What *did* he want?

Suddenly, with the sound of an axe hitting wood, his grandsons succeeded in smashing their skulls together like atoms in a particle collider. Their faces slack with shock, they ran straight across the snowy field, crying "Crampa! Crampa!" and dove tearfully into his welcoming lap. He kissed their crowns to make them better and held them while they sobbed it out. The fullness in his heart made him smile.

When he glanced Claire's way, she wore an identical smile.

Hunter said he'd join his father for the nightly dog walk. Though the day had been overcast, a wind had punished the gray layer, fragmenting it; the stars were almost painfully bright in patches of the dark sky. Winstead and Ruby were much more interested in yellow stains in the snow.

"Be Christmas in a week," Hunter remarked.

Sander agreed this was true.

"How goes it with the widows?" Hunter teased. "Any updates?"

"Had a nice time with Claire after preschool today. She's an interesting person. She says she might be agreeable to something more—of a relationship, I mean—but only if I stop seeing Lucille and Allison and anybody else."

"Ah."

Sander nodded. "I get where she's coming from, I suppose. She tells me she feels like she's on 'The Bachelor.' I don't know what that is."

"I don't either."

"Apparently if you're a woman over fifty in Traverse City, Michigan, you have to watch 'The Bachelor.' From what I gather, some guy's put in a room with a bunch of women and after trying them all out he decides which one he's going to marry."

"Marry? And this is a TV show?"

"Yes, they actually get married, and then they're on the cover of 'People' for six months. It's reality TV."

"So this guy is introduced on camera to a bunch of women, and he has to choose one to marry, and that's *reality*?"

"I kid you not. So Claire says Allison and Lucille are just waiting for me to pick between them. Lucille's trying to, uh, use her charms, and Allison is sort of trying to guilt me into it. Actually, Allison's already ended the relationship twice—it's sort of hard to tell with her."

Hunter laughed. They were rounding the block, heading back home. "Hey," he said suddenly, "I want to thank you for putting out the Christmas decorations. I completely forgot about those."

"Oh, that was Ello," Sander corrected. "I pretty much just did whatever she commanded me to do."

"It's the first Christmas tree we've ever had that we didn't go get as a family," Hunter mused ruefully.

Sander related the story of the burlapped tree that unfolded its limbs in revealed perfection.

Hunter laughed. "That's so Ello. To feel like she has to rescue a tree."

As they walked on, his face turned serious.

"What's happened?" Sander inquired. "What did you just think of, to make you seem sad?"

Hunter shrugged. "You know, Juliana's illness sort of changed everything, but not really. I told you we were having difficulties before. She wants to be back working full-time, which for an attorney is like eighty hours. When she comes home, I think she's still going to be unhappy in the marriage.'"

Sander blew a white cloud into the cold air, nodding. "That makes sense. Whatever was going on with you two will still be there when she recovers."

"I need to win her back, Dad," Hunter declared urgently. "I can't lose her."

"I understand."

"I think the best way to do that is to make this Christmas as perfect as possible. You know how she likes to get all of her details exactly right."

Sander cocked his head. "Really? I don't believe that has anything to do with it, son."

"I have to try *something*."

Sander pondered things for a moment. "You've always been at war with yourself. . . . Did you ever think of that?"

"Not sure I understand."

"I mean that you plan everything, write everything down, because at heart you're a dreamer. Every morning when you leave, I go around the house fetching your coffee cups from all over."

Hunter chuckled sheepishly.

"So you think you can control things if you make all these checklists, but you and Juliana are different. She does it because that's who she is. Look, if you're worried about losing your wife, don't try to be more like her. You need to go back to being the man that she fell in love with in the first place."

Hunter speculatively regarded his father. "It was easier when I was broke. When I didn't have a mortgage and a car payment and children and taxes, but was just struggling to get by after college. She was so beautiful, this Brazilian goddess who looked so different from all the other pasty-faced people here in Michigan. I was trying to figure out how to get close to her. . . . It was this time of year, in fact. And she was singing in a Christmas choir. So I joined it. I was the worst singer in the history of that whole choir. She kept laughing at me. And I knew, if I could just keep her laughing, I could win that girl. But," Hunter confessed mournfully, "there really hasn't been much laughter lately. Her day is such a grind, with the kids, the house. She's a litigator, Dad. It's like I've tied a racehorse to a milk wagon. I have to figure out what I'm going to do about that. Because if I don't, I'm going to lose her for sure."

"You can do it, son. If you're willing to try, you can do it."

"Thanks, Dad."

The dogs picked up their pace, recognizing the scent of home. They had been so excited to go for a walk, and now they were excited for it to be over.

"Hey, you ready for tomorrow?" Hunter asked Sander.

Sander grinned. "I'm ready."

# CHAPTER TWENTY-FOUR

Her first day out of the ICU and in a normal hospital room, Juliana was manic with the idea that she'd be seeing her sons after preschool. It was far too early for their arrival, but she was already awake, excited, unable to sleep. The noise surprised her when Hunter rapped his knuckles on her doorframe and entered, clutching flowers, his posture slightly tense.

Juliana was puzzled. "Hunter?"

He thrust the flowers out in front of him. She was able to move her arms now, and accepted the bouquet, holding it across her body like a beauty contestant. He seemed really nervous.

"What's going on, honey?" she asked, smelling the flowers.

Hunter drew in a breath and began singing the Billy Preston song "You Are So Beautiful." Years of disuse had not improved his singing voice. His rendition sounded like Joe Cocker being bitten by a dog.

She couldn't help but laugh, especially when he got lost in the lyrics and improvised: *"With all that's in our basement, with all that's on our knees . . ."*

Thankfully he kept it short. She clapped at the end. "That was . . . special," she assured him.

"Want to hear another one?"

She winced. "Oh, let's not spoil the mood. I haven't heard you sing in a long time. Do you remember when you started coming to my Christmas choir? I said I'd go out with you to get you to stop."

"I did that?" Hunter replied, his eyes sly.

They were both smiling. Juliana's arms were tube-free, so she raised them. "Come here, husband."

Hunter moved so gently, it was as if he were getting in bed with a pile of loose lightbulbs. Juliana closed her eyes at the feeling of him pressing against her. Everything normal had been yanked away from her, but she was slowly getting it all back. Maybe at some point she would be talking to herself as she folded laundry, and her ennui would re-engage, but at this moment she couldn't imagine anything better than being home with the family, making Sander his perfect fried eggs, driving the kids to school, fixing dinner, and setting a plate aside for Hunter, who would be staying late at the office.

Even better than the flowers was the vanilla milkshake Hunter had brought in from the commissary. She sighed, closing her eyes with the first sip.

"Good?" he asked with a smile.

"You have no idea."

"You ready for the twins?"

Juliana laughed weakly. "It will be fun to see them. Ello says they don't even notice that I'm gone."

Hunter shook his head. "That's not right. They've been very clingy with Ello, and they demand story after story when Dad puts them to bed." He caught her look and nodded. "Oh, yes, my father's been very helpful."

"That's wonderful." Juliana gestured to a sheaf of papers by her side. "Hunter, have you read Ello's essay about Sean O'Brien?"

Hunter looked puzzled. "Essay?"

"She had to pick someone to interview for an assignment, then write a biography. There's a whole section of just facts, like place of birth, and it's pretty detailed. By the time you've gotten all the answers from your interviewee, you know things about the other person that would never occur to you to ask. Not just, 'What's your favorite movie?' but 'Who were you with when you saw your favorite movie?' and 'What's your relationship to that person now?' Then there's the actual bio. Obviously, by the time you've gone through this exercise, you probably know the other person really well, but in this case, there's more. Let me read something to you." Juliana picked up the papers and adjusted them. "'Sean has moved several times because of his mother's career, but he always has a cool attitude about it. Most kids would hate relocating, but that's not his deal. He makes friends because he's always smiling and nice to everyone. He's also mature and cares about being a good person in the world. People like being around him. He's athletic and strong and all the girls think he's hunky.'" Juliana set the papers down. "Our little girl's in love, Hunter."

Hunter blinked. "What? No. You got all that from this assignment?"

"Does she talk about him to you at all?"

Hunter shook his head. "No. Never."

"So she's been gathering all this data—there's a lot of it—and forming these impressions of this boy, and she's never once mentioned him to her father? Then, yes, she's fallen in love."

"She's awfully young for that," Hunter objected. "I mean, love, that's a pretty strong word. She's only in eighth grade. I haven't even *met* this boy! I don't think a daughter should be running around falling in love with some boy without the father being involved. Do you?"

"Oh, Hunter."

Her husband began to pace the room. "This is my fault, but I can fix it. I've been so distracted. She just has no idea what teenage boys are like." He stopped and gave Juliana a determined gaze. "Should we take away her cell phone?"

"You're going to try to confiscate her cell phone just because she has a boyfriend? I'd rather stick my head in a badger hole."

"Boyfriend? First you said she's in love, has a crush, likes a boy, now he's her boyfriend? This is going way too fast!"

Juliana sighed, smiling.

"She's just a child. A little girl! Remember at the zoo when she got lost for only ten seconds, how relieved she was when I found her?"

"Hunter, that was five years ago."

"Well. No."

"No?"

"I mean, no to the boyfriend, no to the love, no to the whole thing. Aren't there girls' schools, or something?"

"You told me you fell in love with Susie somebody in seventh grade. How is this any different?"

"Well sure, seventh grade." He considered his answer, then nodded, apparently conceding the point. "Okay. I mean, no dates or anything, but okay. After he comes over and talks to me."

Juliana laughed delightedly. "You're killing me here."

Hunter grinned back at her. "Oh, man."

"What?"

"I just . . ." Hunter swallowed, his eyes suddenly moist. "There was a time there, for a while, when I wasn't sure I'd ever hear you laugh again."

Juliana reached out a hand and he took it. She felt his need and his love flowing through his grip, and a warm, mellow calm settled over her. They sat like that for a long while, comfortably silent.

"Might be a tad awkward if Ello's boyfriend's mother is my boss," Hunter mentioned.

"How *is* work?" she asked.

"Oh. You know. Fine. A hassle."

She picked up something in the way he answered—he was almost too dismissive. Her inner alarm told her something was going on. Hunter always wanted to talk about work. "Was the installation everything you hoped it would be?" she probed.

"Even more," Hunter avowed.

Which meant things might be changing for them soon. That was why he looked uncomfortable. "Has there been anything definite on the promotion?" she inquired delicately.

Hunter shook his head. "Not yet. Topic hasn't come up. I imagine Mrs. O'Brien will want to speak to me after holiday break."

Juliana nodded. "I want you to know, I'll support whatever you want to do. I mean it. If you're on the road, I can deal with it. As long as I have you, I can deal with anything."

His smile was soft and loving, as was his kiss.

He was only out the door for a moment when he stuck his head back in her room. "Wait a minute," he said. "Go back. What were the rules for Ello's assignment?"

Sander dropped the kids off at preschool, then sat in the minivan, watching cars drive up, dump children, and drive off. He was lingering to see if Claire showed up. She'd said they went ahead and signed up her grandchild Jenner to attend here. Sander was looking sharp in his suit and hoping she'd see him. When the last car had departed and he was alone, he had to face the fact that he had missed her.

Sander reached for his cell phone and carefully tapped his thumbs on the screen.

SG: Hello Claire. I am at the preschool. I was hoping to run into you today. Did I arrive too late?

He waited for a few moments before her reply.

CT: I don't text.

Laughing, he pushed CALL.

Ello watched Sean saunter up to her as the school announced the end of first period with a cascade of locker slammings. "Hey!"

"Hi," she responded cautiously. *What's going on?* she wanted to ask him, but of course never would.

"Cool how much more it snows here than in Detroit."

"Uh-huh." *So now we're going to talk about the weather?*

"Haven't seen you much," he observed, and the first signs that maybe Something Was Wrong flickered across his face like a warning beacon.

"I noticed," she responded flatly, because although they were in the same classes and had the same lunch, he'd been acting like she was invisible.

*Are you mad at me?*

Sean's smile had completely left the building. His eyes were searching hers now. "I mean," he began softly, "the thing with your dad that I told you. Is it, like, a thing now between us?"

"What? No, of course not."

*What about your mother's rage mode? Is that a thing between us?*

"Okay, because I was worried you might be mad at me."

"Because of that? No." *You obviously have never seen me mad.*

"Oh, good." He sighed, then smiled again.

"I mean, it's kind of the worst, because my dad's acting like nothing's wrong." A tremor passed through Ello as she reflected on her father's brave face, covering his concern to protect his family.

"You okay?" Sean asked, looking ready to take another three-day suspension for her.

She nodded. "Yeah, I'm good."

"So we're still friends then."

Ello nodded. *Friends.*

After visiting Juliana, Hunter returned to his office. There was a large envelope sitting on his desk, his name printed across the front. He opened it and scanned the document inside. It was brief and to the point: as of the second of January, he was fired. He would receive his accumulated vacation pay and two weeks' severance. Valerie O'Brien had written a note by hand to him at the bottom. It didn't say, *Thanks for your years of hard work,* or, *Really appreciate all the extra unpaid hours you put in.* It said, *Maybe it would be best for you to pack up your things for Christmas break and just not come back.*

Kim stuck her head in his door. "I texted, then I called your cell phone," she accused.

Hunter patted his pockets with a frown.

"The fire marshal's here to do a surprise inspection. Were you expecting him? It's not in my calendar."

"I don't think they schedule surprise inspections," Hunter replied mildly.

"I do all the work and nobody thanks me, and then we have a surprise fireman," she scolded. "I'm barely keeping this place running as it is."

"I agree with that," Hunter allowed, but Kim didn't seem to hear. He followed her out to the reception area. A man in a suit with white, trimmed hair and a determined look on his face was waiting for him at the front desk, his posture stern and combative.

"Mr. Goss? I'm the fire marshal." The man flipped open a wallet with a fire-department badge in it. He showed it to Hunter, Kim, and the man fixing the drinking fountain. "Fire marshal," he repeated. "This is a surprise inspection."

"Why don't we take the elevator upstairs," Hunter suggested. He led the way. Once he was alone with the fire marshal in the lift, he grinned. "Maybe tone it down just a little, Dad."

Sander winked.

They strolled out into Cardboard Central. Even in the middle of the room, where the employees had always sat back-to-back, a Great Wall of China had been erected. Sander's mouth dropped open at the sight.

Hunter let Sander take the lead, while engineer eyes peered through cut-out holes and tracked their progress. His father spent a lot of time nodding at the sprinklers and the smoke detectors. "All that's pretty good, but what's with this cardboard?"

Hunter had steered his father near one of the main

proponents of the box rebellion, Matthew Danner. Matthew had dark eyes and hair, and avoided other people and shampoo in the same measure. Matthew didn't turn around, even as the two Goss men stopped directly behind his chair.

"You'll have to ask them. This is Matthew Danner."

Matthew didn't turn around.

"Matthew," Hunter prodded gently, "the fire marshal would like to speak to you."

Matthew still didn't turn around.

"You going to pay attention, or get a citation for refusing to assist in a government investigation?" Sander demanded with heat.

When Matthew swiveled in his chair, Sander opened his badge wallet, then flipped it shut with a *snap*. "What's with the cardboard, son?"

Matthew blinked rapidly. "We put them up because the new furniture doesn't have walls."

Hunter saw that their performance had captured the attention of almost every eyeball in the peepholes.

"I see." Sander surveyed the room. "All right, then," he called loudly. "Attention, please. How many of you want to keep your boxes up?"

Hands poked up over the barriers.

"Every single one of you then. Okay." Sander turned to Hunter. "Since it's your first offense, I will only fine you a thousand dollars. Today. It increases to five thousand when I come back tomorrow. For the company, and," Sander raised his voice, "each of you individually."

Matthew's eyes bulged. "Wait, *what*?"

Sander pulled out the ticket book they'd purchased from Staples on the way to the office. "I'll need each of you to have your driver's license out when I come by to issue you your one-thousand-dollar personal fine for creating a public safety danger to the public," he proclaimed loudly.

Matthew looked panicked.

"Identification, please, son?" Sander asked pleasantly.

"Wait! No. I'm—I was just going to take it down!"

Sander paused from writing—Hunter could see the words GREASY HAIR—and regarded Matthew warily.

"Seriously," Matthew babbled. He began ripping at the cardboard, the tape yielding with reluctance.

Sander nodded his fire-marshal approval and pushed past more cardboard to the next engineer in the row. "Your name?"

With that, the room exploded into action, the walls coming down like Jericho's. Hunter watched approvingly as the barriers were flattened, the engineers stomping and ripping. Then he felt a touch at his elbow. It was Kim.

"Hunter? The fire marshal's here."

Hunter nodded and pointed. "Yep."

Kim shook her head. "No, I mean another one."

# CHAPTER TWENTY-FIVE

An unsmiling African-American man, well-muscled and equipped with a strong handshake, greeted Hunter in the lobby. "Mr. Goss? They tell me you're the director of facilities. I am William Anthony Gary, fire inspector."

"Yes, sir," Hunter replied faintly.

"Don't look so alarmed—this is all routine. We always stop by after a building is refitted with new furniture, make sure the tenant hasn't accidentally moved a fire extinguisher or dismantled a smoke detector, that sort of thing."

"Let's start on the lower floor," Hunter suggested.

He stalled the best he could, nearly doing a fist pump when Officer Gary accepted a cup of coffee in the break room. Hunter prepared a cup for him as deliberately as a lab worker transferring Ebola samples. But then, of course, just as Hunter was trying to divert the man's attention to the neat pyramid of Kim's herbal tea boxes, Sander strolled in with a wide grin on his face.

"They're all done," he advised gleefully.

"Well, thank you very much for stopping by today,"

Hunter said meaningfully to his father. He gestured with his eyes toward the door.

Sander ignored him. He strode forward with his hand stretched out toward Officer Gary. "Afternoon. Name's Captain Sanders. I'm the fire marshal."

Officer Gary looked nonplussed.

"And you are?" Sander prompted.

Hunter cringed.

"William Anthony Gary. Fire department," the man stated, shaking Sander's hand.

Sander looked delighted. "Well, hey! What a coincidence. What do you do for them?"

"Fire Marshal," Officer Gary answered slowly.

Sander's smile winked out. "Huh."

"Uh, Dad? Why don't you wait out in the car?" Hunter proposed pointedly.

Sander turned a baffled look on his son, as if unsure he'd heard correctly.

"Okay? Wait for me there. In the car."

In a daze, Sander turned and left the room.

Officer Gary had his eyebrows raised. "You want to tell me what that was all about?"

"My dad," Hunter replied, hoping that would be enough of an answer.

"And? He said *he's* the fire marshal."

"Yes, I heard that."

The two men gazed at each other without blinking, for what seemed to Hunter to be a very long moment. "My dad . . ." Hunter began again. Finally, his brain managed to make it out of the ditch. "My dad's, well . . . yesterday, he said he was an astronaut. Before that, he was a beekeeper, and ah, a professional bowler."

Officer Gary watched Hunter expressionlessly.

Hunter shrugged. "I don't see the harm in letting him think, you know, that he's somebody besides just a grandpa."

Kim had entered, holding Hunter's cell phone with an outstretched hand. "It was on top of the filing cabinet," she accused him.

"Thanks." Hunter gave her the same please-leave signal with his eyes, but Kim stood fast.

"The fire marshal left. The other one," she announced carefully, giving Officer Gary a significant glance.

"Right. The 'other one,'" Hunter replied with air quotes, giving Kim an exaggerated wink. She glared back at him in outrage.

"Seemed like a real nice guy," Officer Gary offered.

Kim shook her head in disbelief.

❄

Hunter slid into the minivan. Sander, behind the wheel, was in high spirits.

"That was the most fun I've had in a long time," he chuckled. "You see the expression on their faces when I told them about the fines?"

"You did a great job, Dad. Perfect."

"Was that really the fire marshal?"

"Yeah."

"Well, that was an awkward moment."

They both laughed. "I told him you were addled," Hunter explained. "That you think you're a dance instructor and the ambassador to France."

They laughed some more, and Sander eyed his son curiously when Hunter's mirth suddenly cut short, as if he had shut a door on it. "What is it?"

Hunter shrugged. "The cardboard's gone, but that doesn't mean the new configuration's going to work. They're all fighting the idea of getting to know each other, especially if it's being forced on them. You ask one of them anything personal about another, and they know absolutely nothing. And that's how they want it. Other than knowing how they code, they have no interest in their fellow humans."

"You'll think of something."

"Well, I do have an idea, actually. Not sure it will work, but it's sort of the only shot I've got. I mean, it should work, but only if I can motivate them to cooperate. Haven't been very good at that particular endeavor lately." Hunter peered at the blank glass face of the office building. "I think I'll go see Juliana."

"Good idea," Sander agreed. "Oh, and Hunter: no need to set a place at the dinner table for me tonight. Ello and I put together a *ropa vieja* in the slow cooker. You can let me know if we got it right."

Hunter regarded his father. "Wait, go back. No need to set a place. . . . Which widow we talking about?"

Sander smiled. "Claire."

Hunter nodded thoughtfully. "Isn't she the one who says she doesn't want to get involved with you unless you ditch the harem?"

"Harem," Sander snorted. "Hardly. Yep, that's her. We're seeing each other, but just as friends. I really enjoy her company."

Hunter's mind was on something else. "What do you think that car of yours is worth?"

Sander looked at his son in surprise. "Why on earth would you want it?"

"I work with software geeks. They *love* things like that. Classic car, perfect condition. Probably would be even more exciting to them that it *doesn't* have an engine," Hunter explained. "And think about it. When those guys were kids, a Monte Carlo driving by with its top down had to be just about the coolest thing on the road."

"And?"

Hunter smiled. "I think I just suddenly figured out the second piece of the puzzle."

"Second piece? How many pieces are there?"

Hunter hesitated. "Well, two."

"Doesn't sound like much of a puzzle to me."

"You willing to sell me your car? Use the money to get a Ferrari, have your face lifted, go on Tinder?"

Sander laughed. "Not a Ferrari, no plastic surgery, and no tenderizer. You want the car? It's yours."

❄

Ello stared at the ceiling above her bed, Ruby's head on her chest. The dog was sound asleep. She was talking on the phone with Siouxanne, who was new to the school this year and had been frozen out by Brittne. It turned out they had a lot in common. They dressed similarly, but not too alike. They both read dog books. They both thought Traverse City sucked in the winter but loved how the lights on Front Street looked at Christmas.

"I hope I got him the right thing," Ello agonized. "I mean, what do I know about hockey? I read that Gordie Howe was pretty good, but that was a long time ago."

Siouxanne cracked an audible bubble out of her gum. "Well, if he doesn't care about the guy, could he just wear it?"

"Maybe. . . . It's pretty big."

"He'll love it."

"I just want him to know I'm not all, like, we're boyfriend and girlfriend. We're just friends and I got him a Christmas gift. No big deal."

"You see Brittne's jeans with the slits up the calf? What's up with that?" Siouxanne demanded.

Ello stroked Ruby's silken ears. "I don't care what Brittne does."

Maybe that was true.

Though his passion was in full boil, it was Sander who broke away from Claire, not the other way around. They were just saying goodnight on her doorstep, and even though he had not submitted a formal petition for permission, moving in for a smooch to cap off their date had seemed as natural as anything in the world. But it lasted longer and became far more ambitious than Sander had intended.

They grinned at each other when they parted. "That wasn't exactly a just-friends kiss," Sander observed wryly.

"I won't tell if you won't."

"I'm just attempting to honor the terms of our agreement."

"Me too," she admitted. "But you seem to have skills that I underestimated in this department, Sander Goss." She cocked her head at him. "Of course, there are other ways to stay within the guidelines."

"I do understand what you are saying to me here, Claire." Though truthfully, Claire was being less than clear.

Her eyes sparkled. "Do you? I'm suggesting that, every single time, quality beats quantity."

Before he could think of a response, Claire gave him a goodnight peck and turned away, slipping quietly into her house. Sander remained on the doorstep, his breath billowing out in ephemeral clouds, his mind lingering on their kiss.

When Allison texted him, he ignored it.

One morning Winstead was distressed because Daddy had pulled the tarp off of the car, but they weren't going for a car ride. The garage door was open, but Winstead was restrained by a leash and unable to bound out into the snow in the front yard, and that didn't make him happy either.

He barked when a rattling truck backed up the driveway. Daddy patted Winstead's muzzle and tied the leash to the workbench. Then Daddy and Hunter and a stranger pushed the car, grunting as they did so, which was followed by the sounds of chains clinking and a machine whining.

Still imagining the rich odors and comforting motion of Daddy's car, Winstead was astonished and alarmed when the noisy truck bumped off down the driveway and Daddy's car followed it, canted up into the air. Not understanding any of this, Winstead wagged and yawned. Hunter slid into his own vehicle and followed the loud truck, but Daddy remained behind.

Winstead picked up on Daddy's sadness and nosed his leg in concern.

"We sure put a lot of wonderful miles on that odometer, didn't we, Winstead?" Daddy whispered.

Winstead wagged. *Where did the car go? What are we doing?*

"Things change, buddy." Daddy stroked Winstead's head. "You can fight it and be defeated by it, or you can embrace it. Right?"

Winstead remained unhappy. He wanted to go for a car ride.

Daddy slapped his hands together with a muffled, gloved impact. "How 'bout we go for a walk?"

*Walk! Even better!*

❄

Ruby was frantic. She put her front paws on the back of the couch and watched in berserk alarm as Winstead and Sander headed down the sidewalk, clearly taking a walk without her!

The house was completely empty. Ruby whined and ran to Winstead's bed, but of course Winstead wasn't in it. Ello was not in her room. The twins were gone, too, and attacking a toy offered Ruby no comfort whatsoever.

Distraught, Ruby could only think of one thing to do, which was to go to Sander's closet, pull out a shoe, and chew it. Then she ripped apart a magazine that had been left on the floor next to his chair. Then she returned to her post at the window. She was alone. Abandoned. They had forgotten all about her!

She managed to gnaw a hole in Winstead's bed and yank tufts of material out, hating the way the stuff clung to her tongue, but unable, under these emergency conditions, to stop.

Finally the door squeaked and banged and Ruby tore through the house. Sander was stomping his feet as he unclipped Winstead's leash. Ruby frantically leapt on Winstead, who sniffed back suspiciously. She put up her paws and tried to jump up to Sander's face.

"Yes, hello Ruby, good dog," he greeted her gruffly.

Obviously sensing trouble, Winstead padded back to

Sander's bedroom, and Ruby followed. The big dog put his nose to the tumbleweeds of bed stuffing strewn on the floor. He was not wagging.

Sander entered the room and pulled up short at the mayhem. Winstead looked up at him guiltily.

"Oh, Ruby," Sander muttered mournfully.

Monty met Hunter at the double doors at the end of the atrium in Hunter's building. His two helpers swiftly pulled the pins on the hinges, frigid air swirling around their feet as they pushed the Monte Carlo into the center of the room, where anyone standing at the windows on all four sides of the five-story chamber could see the incongruous sight.

Kim gaped at him. "You can't park a car in the building."

"Well, actually, I can," Hunter replied, watching Monty and his men efficiently return the doors to their places.

Kim threw her hands in the air. "I need a mental health break."

Hunter was polishing the car's finish to a gleam when he saw Kim, in coat and hat, stalk out the door and into the cold day. He sighed and called up to the executive floor to have their assistant come down to cover the main reception desk. Then he stood, waiting, watching the windows above him.

It was like opening a can of tuna in a house full of feral

cats. One by one, the software engineers pressed against the glass and stared down as if Hunter were an exotic zoo animal. Gradually, they drifted into the atrium.

Hunter grinned at them as they gathered around the classic automobile.

# CHAPTER TWENTY-SIX

S ander's baby-blue convertible had its top down and its hood open to expose a clean, empty engine compartment. By Hunter's reckoning, every software geek in the company had been lured down to admire the thing. Hunter stood on the Monte Carlo's back seat, taking in their expressions.

"This is a 1980 Chevrolet Monte Carlo. It's a classic. We're having a contest, and the winner gets the car."

They all stared in amazement.

"So here's how to play. You'll find printed forms in all the common areas, including right there on the table, there."

The geeks immediately snatched up the papers and began examining them critically, like lawyers searching for loopholes in a contract.

"You'll see that there are two sections on each form to fill out. One is basic data—place of birth, number of children, all that. The second section is an essay for writing out the biography of the person. A narrative . . . not just dry facts, but the actual story of their lives. The goal is to fill one of these out for every employee in the building. Each form you hand in is an entry into the contest to win this immaculate, classic car. Each biography will be assessed for accuracy and awarded points. So the person who completes the most accurate entries will win the car. Simple."

He could tell by their expressions that nobody thought it was simple. Hands shot up. "Stephen?" Hunter called.

"So what if someone sabotages you by giving you all wrong answers?"

"Well," reasoned another engineer before Hunter opened his mouth, "if you lie to everyone, your lie becomes the truth. If you say to everyone you were born in Cuba, then it doesn't matter where you were born in reality, because you said to everybody it was Cuba."

"Cuba," someone snorted derisively.

"So why not lie inconsistently?" another coder objected.

That stumped the others for a minute.

"Okay, well, you're going to have to be talking to each other anyway," Hunter reasoned. "You could compare answers. If Gordon says he was born in Cuba to one person and Canada to another, you'll know he's lying."

"And if someone lies, we'll freeze him out," Gordon declared triumphantly. "No one will talk to him. He won't be able to do any entries of his own."

"So there's an incentive to be truthful and to talk to as many people as possible," Hunter concluded with satisfaction.

"Is accurate the right word, though? What about completeness?" someone challenged.

"Or creativity?"

"Readability?"

"Not creativity," someone jeered.

Hunter was smiling. *Engineers.* "Sure," he replied noncommittally.

When he left the atrium, everyone was buzzing, but it soon proved to be difficult to write while standing. Eventually they moved upstairs, where the furniture was configured to make consulting with one another more convenient.

Sander grunted as he lifted Barbara's urn from its shelf. He carried it tenderly, holding it as if it were an infant as he moved to his chair. When he sat, he put his arms around it, hugging her to his chest. For a long moment, he sat silently while Winstead folded his lanky limbs and collapsed into his bed.

"Hey, Barbara," Sander murmured. Winstead flicked his eye open at the words. "I have something I need to talk to you about." He sighed and, when he spoke again, his throat hurt. "Remember in the hospital when I was reading to you and you interrupted me and told me you wanted me to get married again? You said you knew I loved you, but this was death-do-us-part, so I was released from my wedding vows. And I said no, I could never love anyone else. I only have room in my heart for one woman. Well, that's true, Barbara. I love you and I will never love anyone else the same way. But I've met someone, and . . ."

Sander closed his eyes. What was he really doing? He was holding his wife, the woman he had loved forever, trying to explain something that had only recently occurred to him: one's heart could grow bigger and make room for someone else without evicting the former tenant.

Finally, Sander leaned forward and tenderly touched the smooth surface of the urn with his lips.

Juliana was reading in her hospital bed when Hunter came in. He bent down for a kiss and she pulled him close to prevent him from making it perfunctory. When he drew back, they were both smiling.

"How is the patient today?"

"I keep telling them I'm well enough to go home. I mean, I'm off dialysis and everything, and they keep saying I have to stay for a few more days. Looks like I'm going to miss Christmas."

Hunter shook his head. "Oh, no. We wouldn't have Christmas morning without you, honey."

Juliana frowned, picturing her children getting up for Christmas and not being allowed to unwrap their gifts. *Did Santa Claus skip our house?* What explanation could they offer the twins for why December 25th wasn't a holiday this year? "That wouldn't be right, Hunter. Let's not ruin Christmas for them. No, I'll be fine."

"Ruin Christmas . . ." Hunter repeated.

"Just set my gifts aside. I'll open them when I'm home. Probably the 27th, they're telling me."

"You sure?"

"Okay, no. Not completely. But I don't want them believing I've chosen the hospital over the family."

"Well, they're only three. They'll probably recover from the trauma pretty quickly. Your decision, though."

"Let's not ruin Christmas."

"Okay," Hunter agreed. "Let's not ruin Christmas."

Sander stood when he saw Lucille sweep through the doors of the restaurant. He waved at her and she beamed at him, handing her fur coat to the hostess.

Her hair was carefully done, loose curls falling to her shoulders, and her eyes were particularly vivacious—some makeup thing, he supposed. When she reached him, her momentum carried her right into his arms and he returned her kiss as if they were alone. When she broke away, eyes sparkling, she did a little twirl in front of him. "You like?"

Her black skirt was lacy and flowing, and her blouse managed to resemble lingerie. Her cleavage was coyly on display in a material that tricked the eye into seeing more than was actually revealed. Sander allowed himself to linger in his examination because she was, after all, asking for his studied opinion. "I like it very much. You look beautiful, Lucille."

She nodded her approval at his response, allowing him to pull her chair back and seat her. "I wanted to dress for the occasion."

He sat. "Occasion?"

She gestured around the room. They were in a small, intimate restaurant atop a hotel built in 1930.

"I thought maybe you brought me here for a reason." She reached out and traced his knuckles with a fingertip. "I hope you don't have to rush back to your home tonight, Sander. I thought we could go to my place for a little dessert." She looked up at the approaching waiter. "I think I'd like champagne."

Sander ordered himself an iced tea. Lucille gave him a questioning look, but he simply turned and gazed out into the night, the small town glittering with festive lights that threw soft puffs of diffused color onto the snow.

"You like driving, Lucille? Just getting in the car, cruising out into the country, looking at the woods, the fields?"

"I'd drive anywhere with you."

"That was something Barbara loved to do."

She reacted warily, not sure what he was saying. "I won't be able to compete with your dead wife, Sander," she finally whispered.

He shook his head. "I would never ask anyone to do that."

"I'm my own person."

"No doubt in my mind."

She leaned forward, regarding him intently. "I have a feeling we're about to have a very important conversation."

Winstead did not understand what was happening, and it made him nervous.

First: this new car. Why weren't they in Daddy's old car? Or alternatively, the big minivan with the children and Ruby? Now it was Winstead alone in the back with no additional seats behind him, only a small space. As much as he preferred to have Daddy to himself, this change in routine felt deeply disquieting.

His anxiety increased when Daddy stopped the car. There was something in the way Daddy turned and looked at him that suggested to Winstead he was about to be abandoned.

"I'll be right back, buddy," Daddy assured him.

And with that, the absolute worst thing happened: his person eased out of the vehicle and shut the door without taking Winstead with him. Winstead watched in near panic as Daddy strolled up a short sidewalk and knocked on a door. Within moments, the door opened and Daddy disappeared inside.

Winstead paced back and forth on the back seat, as if looking out one window would give him different information than the other. He yawned and painted marks on the glass with his nose. He jumped over his seat into the space behind it and then immediately jumped back. He sat, trying to be good, and then barked, no longer caring.

He wagged in relief when, after what seemed an interminable length of time, his person reappeared out of that same door, trailed by a woman whose movements seemed familiar.

When Daddy opened the door opposite the steering wheel, the interior of the vehicle filled with the woman's flowery scent. She slid into her seat and looked around in admiration.

Winstead anxiously tracked Daddy as he walked around the front of the car. When the driver's side door opened and he finally climbed in, Winstead was almost frantic with gratitude. He leaned forward to lick Daddy's ear, but his person dodged his head away.

"My, my, Mr. Goss," the woman commented. "A Porsche? I didn't even know they made an SUV."

"Well, I needed a back seat for the grandboys, and I simply had to escape that minivan. It was reducing my testosterone levels."

The woman laughed and twisted in her seat. "Hello, Winstead."

Winstead identified the essential smell that was this woman, barely discernible under the billowing clouds of perfume wafting from her. He recognized the odor from a place where Daddy often took him and Ruby and the twins to play. Winstead wagged uncertainly. He had no idea why they were in the car in the first place, and he was equally unsure why this woman had come with them. He sat alertly as they pulled away from the curb.

"I imagine," the woman observed, "the minivan probably did put a damper on your ability to impress girls."

Daddy laughed. "Girls," he repeated. He glanced at her. "There's only one girl I'm trying to impress now, Claire."

The woman cocked her head. "Oh?"

"That's right."

"So you've decided on one of us? Is this the last episode of 'The Bachelor'? May I ask who the lucky winner is?"

"Me," Daddy responded. "I'm the lucky one."

They drove silently for a while. When Claire reached out and touched Daddy's shoulder, Winstead finally understood why she was in the car.

"Happy Christmas Eve Eve," Hunter greeted Kim.

She gave him a glum look. "We shouldn't have to work today. It's a holiday."

"Actually, it isn't."

"It's unfair."

"Okay, sure."

"The boss wants to see you."

Hunter considered that, nodded.

Something seemed strange about Mrs. O'Brien when Hunter poked his head in her door. It took him a minute to figure out what it was: she was smiling.

"You asked to see me, Mrs. O'Brien?" Hunter asked cautiously.

She shook her head. "Call me Valerie."

What was this? Had she been visited by three ghosts last night?

"Why don't you sit down," she suggested.

Hunter settled warily into his chair. He thought fleetingly about how convicted criminals were offered a final cigarette before the firing squad did their work.

"You know, I've had my doubts about everything you've been doing, but I have to say, this contest of yours has really turned things around. My staff tells me that everyone seems to know so much about each other now."

Hunter nodded. "Turns out we have three college-level volleyball players in our ranks, along with several who played in high school. Who knew? I hear they're putting together a team."

"And I heard from sales that two of the engineers are going bowling with them over the holidays."

Hunter nodded silently, unsure where this was going.

"I'll admit, when those cardboard boxes went up, I thought your career was over and that you were taking me down with you. But now it seems everything's on the right track. It'll be some time before we see whether or not there's any sort of improvement in productivity, but from what I've heard from my peers in this industry, if you can get your engineers working harmoniously, it makes all the difference. Congratulations, Hunter," she continued, beaming. "I've made my recommendation, and it's sure to be accepted. After the first of the year, you'll be the director of facilities for all company operations. I've prepared your compensation package, and I think you'll be pleased." She tapped a thin folder on her desk, then leaned forward and lowered her voice. "I'm going to need your help going forward. There's a lot of fat in our operation. Too many branches—three in California alone. We need to consolidate, reduce head count. You'll be my go-to for all of it."

Hunter stared numbly. "Huh," he said.

❄

Christmas morning.

Hunter eased the minivan to a halt in the hospital parking lot. He shut off the engine and turned to look at his family. "Okay, guys," he enthused. "We ready for this?"

Ello was holding the soft-sided duffel bag in her lap. Inside, Ruby was wiggling and kept thrusting her head through the partially unzipped top.

"The puppy just needs to be quiet until we're past the front desk," Hunter told her.

Ello nodded, clearly tense.

"Am I doing the right thing here," Hunter asked his father, "or am I teaching my children it's okay to be outlaws?" He glanced at the twins. In many ways, they already were outlaws.

"It's a puppy at Christmas," Sander argued. "No one should have a rule against that, not even a hospital."

"The woman at the front counter scares me a little," Hunter admitted.

"Time to man up, Dad," Ello advised.

"Go see Mommy!" Ewan said, his pronunciation so clear that everyone stared at him.

"All right," declared Sander. "Let's do this."

# CHAPTER TWENTY-SEVEN

The Plan To Ruin Christmas had been hatched almost entirely by Ello. She wrote the whole thing down, printed it, and handed it out, which touched Hunter more than he could ever tell her.

Sander was in the far back of the minivan with Winstead, his sunglasses an odd, ridiculous shade of black.

Garrett announced, "We bapa crapa gassa."

Hunter frowned.

"That's right," Sander agreed. "You painted grandpa's glasses. And I can't see a thing."

Winstead, wearing a bright yellow service-dog vest with a harness, was wagging, ready to do whatever it was they were doing.

"You first, Grandpa," Ello directed managerially.

Sander groped his way out of the car, gripping Winstead's harness and trying to see under his glasses. Winstead dragged him over to a parking sign and lifted his leg.

"Even guide dogs have to pee," Ello reasoned.

The twins thought this was hilarious.

As soon as the hospital's front door shut on his father

and Winstead, Ello readied the rest of the family: "Let's do this!"

They jumped out of the car, Ello zipping up her duffel bag. She held it under one arm like a football. The boys followed obediently across the parking lot and into the front lobby.

Sander was at the front desk, cocking his head skyward with a smile. "Merry Christmas," he announced to the receptionist's ceiling. "I brought you a gift!"

With that, he tossed a wrapped box onto the desk with enough force and inaccuracy that it skidded across the surface like a flat rock on a still pond, falling to the floor. The receptionist, already thrown off-kilter, bent to pick up the package. As she did so, Ello hurried past her and down the hall toward her mother's room, Ruby silent in the bag.

When the woman sat back up, she was visibly flustered.

Hunter waved at her as he passed, the twins bumping into his calves. "Just me, Hunter Goss, and my two boys going to visit their mother. That okay?"

The woman nodded, typing his arrival into her computer, then turned to unwrap the gift. "My, this is nice," she proclaimed, surprised. It was chocolates. According to Sander, a woman would accept a gift of chocolates from anyone, no matter how inappropriate.

Hunter and the boys joined Ello in front of the door to their mother's hospital room. Soon, Sander came sauntering around the corner, Winstead's nails clicking on the slick floor beside him.

"That was fun. I read about this one guy who went into professional acting when he was seventy. . . ." he mused.

Hunter nodded. "Okay, maybe by the time you're seventy you'll be able to act. Everyone good to go?"

Juliana gasped in surprise as her entire family came bursting, SWAT-like, through the door.

"Merry Christmas!" Ello announced.

The boys threw themselves on the bed and climbed onto their mother, saying, "Mewwy Cissma."

Winstead put his paws up and sniffed her while Sander took off his sunglasses and blinked in the harsh light.

Juliana hugged her boys, then glanced at her husband. "I didn't know dogs were allowed."

For some reason, this made Ello, Sander, and Hunter laugh out loud. "Get down, boys," Sander commanded. "Give your mother some breathing room."

"We have a new member of the family," Hunter informed her gaily.

While Juliana stared at him in noncomprehension, Hunter nodded at their daughter and Ello lifted the duffel bag onto the bed. She unzipped it and, to Juliana's shock, out bounded a white and brown puppy who made a beeline for Juliana, kissing, kissing, kissing the patient's face.

Juliana peered in confusion at her husband.

He shrugged. "Long story."

At the bottom of the bag were some small gifts. The twins were delighted to receive rubber balls, which they started throwing against the walls. This tantalized Ruby, who jumped off the bed and began chasing them, her legs sliding out from underneath her. Winstead, still in character as a service dog, watched tolerantly. Within seconds, the bedlam had reached crisis level.

"Boys!" Sander commanded sharply.

In Juliana's experience, nothing short of firing a gun into the air would get the twins' attention, so she was shocked when Ewan and Garrett looked up at Sander in surprise.

"Let's play dead-animal-by-the-side-of-the-road," her father-in-law suggested.

It was genius. Upon his command, both boys fell to their backs on the floor, trying to be silent as they giggled, their limbs extended at awkward angles. Sander bent and examined Garrett. "What have we here?" he mused. "A dead elephant? Did somebody driving a Prius hit an elephant?" He reached out and touched Garrett's nose and both boys giggled more loudly. "No," Sander concluded. "An elephant has a big nose. This little squirt has a tiny nose. Maybe it's a sparrow."

Ello had gathered up Ruby and was hugging the dog and kissing her face. Juliana saw the love radiating between them.

*So this is what happens when you fall into a coma. . . . Your daughter talks your husband into getting a puppy.*

"Maybe it's an ostrich!" Sander exclaimed.

"So," Hunter said, "I was offered that promotion. Direc-tor of facilities for the whole company."

Juliana had expected as much. Something in the way her husband was carrying himself had led her to suspect that he had important news.

Sander turned and looked at Hunter wisely. "Oh?" he asked shrewdly. "And what did you say, when they made that generous offer?"

Hunter shrugged a bit too casually. "I resigned."

Juliana gasped aloud.

Hunter smiled at her. "My wife's about to go back to work full-time as a litigator, which is a labor-intensive job. I need a job where I can be flexible, so I can accommodate her schedule. So . . . you know . . . I'll find something. My skills are in pretty big demand right now, and I could probably do consulting, at least. Until I find the right gig."

Juliana could only stare at her husband in wonder.

Sander picked up Ewan by his feet, the boy hang-ing limply upside down, arms trailing toward the floor. "I think it's a fruit bat," Sander announced. He looked over to Juliana and Hunter. "I can help with the boys. I mean, what good's a grandpa if he can't handle a couple of well-mannered, quiet, obedient twins?"

Ello snorted.

"Hey, guys, do you mind if I talk to my wife for just a minute?" Hunter asked the group.

The boys left with their grandpa, Sander observing that they were probably dead worms. but Ello lingered for a moment. She leaned in close to her mother. "Merry Christmas," she whispered, and surprised Juliana by kissing her on the cheek. "I love you, Mom."

"I love you too, Ello," she replied.

"Thank you for letting me keep my dog. This is the most perfect Christmas ever."

It was a presumptuous statement, but Juliana went with it. "Of course," she agreed simply.

After Ello departed, Hunter reached into the bag that she'd left behind and pulled out an unwrapped gift: it was a thick binder, three rings, filled with what looked to be hundreds of sheets of paper.

"What's that?" Juliana asked.

"It's my official moving plan for my now ex-company. Merry Christmas."

"Oh. How thoughtful."

Hunter grinned. "I just wanted you to see how alike we are. We both think we can control outcomes if we just make a detailed enough list. If our plan's perfect, then everything will come off perfectly, right? Turns out, though, no matter how great your plan is, nothing ever goes the way you think it will. It's how you react to the unexpected challenges of life that really matters."

"Okay. I do get what you're telling me," Juliana said, nodding. "But I *like* making lists."

"With you back to work, running the household will be more my responsibility than yours. And I think you'll find, with me doing that, things won't be quite the same. Christmas won't be the same. It'll be good, but different. If you're able to accept that, I think you'll be happy with the results. It's called life."

"You're the man I love, Hunter."

"You're the woman I love, Juliana."

Juliana sighed. "When I woke up and I couldn't move a muscle, I was so terrified. They told me I'd get better, but how could I know that was true? I just felt paralyzed. And the only thing that got me through it was the fact that you were there to take care of me. Here I'd been thinking that you were so focused on your work that you didn't give a hoot what happened to me, our marriage, or our children. And then I saw it was the opposite. I was wrong, and I know I hurt you with what I said at lunch a couple of weeks ago. I really wish I hadn't done that."

Their kiss was sweet, gentle, and long.

When the minivan pulled into the driveway, Sean O'Brien was sitting on the front steps. He had a package in his hand. Ello's heart began to pound. She put a hand to her mouth.

Hunter stopped the car and they all sat silently for a moment, staring at the boy.

"Hey, uh, Dad, can you like . . . I just need a minute," Ello stammered.

"Sure," Hunter agreed.

She jumped out of the car, holding Ruby, and ran right

past Sean, who gaped at her in surprise. "I'll be right back!" she told him.

She dashed up to her room and grabbed the package she had so carefully wrapped. The gift that would communicate, *We're friends . . . not boyfriend and girlfriend, but really good friends. I really care about you, but not in a way that's, like, me trying to say We Should Be Together or anything.*

Ruby nipped at her heels as she darted back down to the front door, but Ello shoved the puppy aside at the last second and shut Ruby in, ensuring that she'd be alone with Sean.

"So, hey," she panted with forced casualness, shoving the package forward like she was handing off a football. "Merry Christmas."

Sean accepted it and handed her a clumsily wrapped box in return. "Merry Christmas," he repeated. They sat next to each other on the front steps.

He unwrapped his present first, Ello watching tensely. When he pulled out the jersey, he gasped aloud.

"So I looked it up and, like, one of the greatest Red Wing players of all time was this guy, Gordie Howe?" Ello explained. "So, uh, that's his jersey. Number nine."

Sean was grinning, but Sean was always grinning, and Ello couldn't tell if he was happy with it or not. But when Sean threw back his head and laughed with childish delight, Ello knew she'd scored.

"Oh my God, it's perfect," he told her, his dimples positively puckering. "*Mr. Hockey!* This is amazing. I love it!"

Sean held the jersey up to his shoulders. It had to be one of the ugliest garments Ello had ever seen. But all that mattered was that Sean liked it.

"Now you," he urged.

Ello decided as she unwrapped the gift that she did not care what was inside. She'd love it because it was from Sean, and frankly, her best present was the way he'd reacted to the Gordie Howe jersey.

Ello sucked in a breath when she saw what was inside. It was a familiar photograph, one that had hung in her bedroom for several years, and along with it, a letter from Meryl Davis, her idol.

"What I did was, I wrote her publicist and explained how you lost the original letter, and she said—can you believe this?—she remembered writing you the first time! If you read it, you'll see she's really excited that you're still ice dancing."

Ello swallowed, not trusting herself to speak. She finally took in a deep breath and shook her head in wonder. "Sean, this is, like, the best gift ever. It's amazing."

They stared at each other and then Sean leaned forward and, as naturally as could be, put his arm around her and brought her face to his.

Ello had kissed other boys before, but it had never been like this. Never this important, never this tender, never this graceful.

It was the Best Day Of Her Life.

❄

Winstead watched tolerantly as Ruby tore around the room, chasing the balls that the boys were throwing around as hard as they could. A picture frame fell to the floor, an ornament was knocked off the tree, but there was no yelling or shouting from the big people in the room, so Winstead didn't react either.

"Did you mean that, Dad?" Hunter asked. "I mean, about helping? Honestly, I talk a big game, but there's no way I can do what Juliana does. And I really do want to be working, not just for the income, but because I don't think I'm cut out to be a full-time, what do you call it? House husband?"

Daddy nodded, easing into a soft chair while Hunter remained standing. "Of course I meant it. I hate to admit it, but Juliana's illness got me off my ass, and I've never felt better."

They grinned at each other. Garrett threw a rubber ball at his brother's forehead. Ruby attacked Winstead's back legs, and Winstead growled, letting the puppy know he wasn't in the mood. All he wanted was to sit next to Daddy's chair.

"So," Hunter asked slyly, "don't you have a widow or two to visit today?"

Daddy laughed. "Just one."

"Oh, really?"

"Her name's Claire. You'll meet her. I don't know. . . . There's just something special about her."

"I thought you were going to be driving around town in your Porsche, racing kids at the stoplights and picking up women twenty-five years younger."

Daddy shook his head. "Not for me."

They sat quietly for a while. Finally, Hunter leaned toward his father. "Thanks for everything, Dad," he said softly. "You really held this family together when it was going through the worst crisis possible. You helped me when I thought I was going to lose my wife. You helped Ello when I was too wrapped up in everything to give her the attention she needed. And somehow you even learned to communicate with the twins. You saved us."

Winstead sensed a burst of emotion coursing through Daddy. He felt it in the tremble of Daddy's hand. Winstead turned and nosed that hand, trying to help.

Daddy stood. "Come here, son."

Hunter took a step forward and the two men came together in a tight, fierce hug.

Winstead wagged.

Ruby, exhausted from playing with the manic twins, sprawled across Ello's legs. The puppy had long forgotten the house with the angry man and the scared boy—*this* was her home now. The day, with its car rides and the visit to the lady in the bed in the big building, had been filled with bouncing balls and boxes with ribbons. Ruby had ripped up crumpled paper until her mouth was dry, and had chased the boys around and around the room while they held aloft plastic objects and made zooming noises with their mouths.

The puppy had never known such excitement. And now Ruby was happily lying with Ello. Soon the puppy and her person would both be asleep.

It had been a perfect day.

# ACKNOWLEDGMENTS

As a professional storyteller, I supposedly have the ability to map out the beginning, middle, and end of a narrative. Yet as I sit down to write my acknowledgments for *A Dog's Perfect Christmas,* I'm not sure where to start and I have only a hazy idea of where I should stop.

The whole thing feels like the middle, frankly—acknowledging and thanking those people who helped me become the writer I am today. Because, after all, who *didn't* help? Even the kid who beat me up in third grade for winning the spelling bee deserves some recognition, because I learned a lesson from that day, which is that some girls are really tough. Or how about the girl who kissed me for the first time in my life, while I lay on the floor of her basement and howled in fake protest? I certainly learned something from that. (Same girl, by the way. Our relationship was complicated.)

So this is going to be difficult. I suppose it would be easiest just to say, "Thanks everybody," and end it there. Certainly people would appreciate the brevity.

Maybe it would be helpful to map out the history of this book. To do that, I have to start with *A Dog's Purpose,* the first novel I ever had published. It wasn't the first one I ever *wrote*, because I had written nine unpublishable novels prior to that, sort of like teaching yourself to ride a bicycle by falling off of it. Nine times. Anyway, Scott Miller, my agent at Trident Media, worked for two years to find a publisher for what we call "ADP"—my first dog book.

And what a home he found for me. Tor/Forge has published every novel I have written since ADP, for a total of, I think, twenty-one now. So thank you, Scott, for all you have done to make me the author I always wanted to be, my ambition going all the way back to around the age when I was pinned to the basement floor by ruthless kisses. And thank you to the team at Tor/Forge—Linda, Tom, Susan, Sarah, Lucille, Eileen—this feels like the Academy Awards—for helping turn that first book into a publishing phenomenon with over thirteen million copies in print worldwide.

Along the way I published a novella called *The Dogs of Christmas*, a huge success that continues to sell tens of thousands of copies every Christmas. A couple of years ago Linda, my publisher, told me her sales staff would really like another novella. And that's the book you just finished reading: *A Dog's Perfect Christmas*. (The original title was *Untitled Cameron Novel*. I liked it, but some people felt the title just lacked spark.)

Of course, there were lots of steps in between. I want to give special thanks to Kristin Sevick, who read an essay of mine called "Last Dance at the Bus Bar" and suggested to me I should have the confidence to write a novel with the kind of heart and soul and family love as in that essay.

With permission to come from a different place than a dog POV, I set out to pen a story about a family having a huge but completely normal crisis heading into the holidays. That everything changes for them when a puppy comes accidentally bounding into their lives seems to me an entirely logical turn of events.

One of the challenges in writing this novel was getting into the mind of a thirteen-year-old girl. I wasn't able to do that when I was thirteen years old myself, and I sure wasn't able to do it when I had a thirteen-year-old daughter. For help, I turned to the daughter of one of my best friends. David Leinberger let me chat with his daughter Lauren. Thank you, Lauren, for teaching me the vocabulary of middle school so that I didn't have to go back to learn it myself. I like to think of myself as being able to face life's challenges but I'm not doing eighth grade again.

Because I have been typing stories since I was in elementary school, my finger muscles and joints and ligaments are all sort of giving up on me. They wake me up at night to complain about how much they hurt and to warn darkly of Alien Hand Syndrome. So the very first draft of this novel was written via dictation, using an Apogee Electronics microphone with magic elves in it. Thank you everyone at Apogee, especially Marlene Passaro, for the donation of this amazing device, which turns my smartphone into a recording studio. Each chapter, when finished, was sent off electronically to Rev.com. Their work, translating my halting mispronunciations into intelligible text, was key to allowing me to get my work done without sobbing.

Okay, I cried a few times but that was emotional and not based on arthritis.

A couple of drafts into every manuscript I hand it to my wife and business partner, Cathryn Michon, who does a deep dive into the prose to hunt out problems. Who would think that a wife would be good at finding flaws in anything a husband does? Thank you, Cathryn, for your patient and extremely helpful notes. You are instrumental and very attractive.

At some point, an author decides it's time to ship the manuscript off to an editor—usually long after the deadline has passed.

This was the first novel wherein my editor was Ed Statler, who did an absolutely fantastic job helping improve the work I had done. In his words, he "liked this novel more than he thought he would." That is high praise coming from an editor. Usually it's much more common to get something like, "Why do you still believe you are a writer?"

After Ed's work the novel was ready to show other people. More than any other person, Gavin Polone, producer of all of the movies that have been made from my books, has had a tremendous and positive impact on my career. I always send him my manuscripts with the warning that "you probably won't like this one." When he responded, "I adore this book," I felt like I had really accomplished something. Thank you, Gavin, for your support, friendship, and wisdom.

Another early reader was my manager, Sheri Kelton. Sheri has made it her mission in life to see that every single book, short story, and grocery list that I have ever written gets made into filmed entertainment. We are all hoping that *A Dog's Perfect Christmas* will be in theaters one day. If it is, it will be because of people like Sheri. Thank you, Sheri, for always being in my corner.

So far in these acknowledgments I've been doing a pretty good job of tracking this novel from inception to where we are currently, but now things are going to get a little fuzzier and less chronological.

Unfortunately, my mother passed away in November 2019. She never had an opportunity to read this book, but I know she would have absolutely loved it. She had some health problems toward the end, and had trouble, after a stroke, reading books, though novels were her passion for as long as I have known her. I showed her how an ebook could enlarge the type font so that she would have no trouble seeing the letters, and she had been reading *A Dog's Promise* when she suddenly and painlessly passed away. She was my biggest fan and would have received an early reader copy of *A Dog's Perfect Christmas,* so I suppose I am still tracking the chronology. Mom, you have no idea how much I miss you.

My attorney, Steve Younger, together with the aforementioned boxing manager, Sheri, will help shepherd this novel through the legal and dealmaking process of being adapted for the screen. If it sounds difficult it probably is, but yet it is a highly critical function, and so thank you, Steve, for going to law school so I didn't have to. While you were there, you might have run into Hayes Michel my criminal attorney who has thus far managed to fight off extradition. Thank you, Hayes.

Thank you, Olivia Pratt, for swimming toward this sinking ship and taking the helm. The crack team at A Dog's Purpose sends out bookmarks, bookplates, free gifts, and we donate a lot of my books to dog charities. None of that would be possible without Olivia, who operates the "back end" of the office and also takes care of important stuff like making sure I don't forget to get my hair cut and that I take my medication and that I get enough martial arts training to ward off any attacks from third-grade spelling bee losers.

Thank you, Diane Driscoll, for finding Olivia for us.

Jill Enders has kept me social for many years. She helps assist the Secret Group on Facebook in loving their dogs and dog books. She answers questions from readers, such as "When will Bruce get a haircut?" (Answer: ask Olivia.)

And what about that Secret Group? They have done a lot of good work over the years, helping us adopt not shop, save them all, and offering counsel to those of us who have lost our furry friends. They are wonderful people and I owe them a debt of my gratitude.

One of the reasons why I was able to write a book instead of spending all of my time taking care of my mother in her last year of life is because she had such a wonderful support team. Too many people to list here, but thank you to Bob Moran, Rocky Dolan, Mary Ellen Furseth, Tom and Diane Runstrom, Jody and Andy Sherwood, Tim Whims, Patrick Faust, Jerry Sulak, John and Patti Masson, and everyone else who kept her safe those last months.

I often tell elementary school children that I have two evil sisters, and it always gets a laugh. But my sisters aren't evil, they are just crazy. Amy and Julie Cameron have supported my work for a long, long time. Amy writes the CORE compliant study guides for my grown-up books. Julie is a physician who makes sure that her patients all read my novels as part of their treatment. Your support means the world to me.

I also have offspring and grand-offspring who cheer for me. Two out of three of my children carry a gun in their line of work, but the third one is who you should watch for. Thank you to Georgia, Chelsea, Chase, Gage, Eloise, Garrett, Ewan, Gordon, Sadie, Alyssa, and James.

Obviously, Eloise, Ewan, and Garrett in this novel were not given those names by sheer chance.

Families continue to grow, like, say, my waistline. Thanks to my strategic marriage, I now have Evie Michon, Ted Michon, Maria Hjelm, and Jacob, Maya, and Ethan Michon as treasured members in my family. (If you have read ADP, you might recognize a few names here.)

I also have two goddaughters. I would appreciate it, Carolina and Annie, if you would stop growing older. I find it disquieting.

I mentioned the study guides earlier. For my youngreader novels, Judy Robbens writes the study guides. You can find all of them, free for download, at adogspurpose.com.

Special shout-out (I'm literally shouting) to Samantha Dunn, an astoundingly talented writer who has encouraged and helped me the whole way.

Sometimes you have friends who support you and though they have no direct impact on your career, they nonetheless are part of what makes it all work. So thanks to Aaron Mendelsohn, Gary Goldstein, Ken Pisani, Mike Conley, Susan Walter, Margaret Howell, Felicia Meyer, and Mike Walker for supporting me as the worst secretary of any organization in history.

Thank you, Dennis Quaid, for standing up for the movie *A Dog's Purpose* when it was under terrorist attack. You are a true mensch, a real Dennissance Man.

I started to name my most treasured friends, and the list started to feel like when during the Academy Awards the person keeps talking even when the music gets loud and two tough women come out to beat him up for winning the spelling bee. I deleted the list maybe thirty people into it. To quote Sharon Solfest in the movie *Cook Off!*, "You know who you are!"

Over the years I have worked with and donated to more than three hundred animal rescue charities, but I want to specifically call out Best Friends and Life is Better Rescue for their tireless work saving animals who need extra human help.

Naming just two animal rescue organizations when there are so many doing such good work feels like I am running a real risk. So many of them do excellent work. So probably this is a good place to stop.

I've just sent the final copy edit of *A Dog's Perfect Christmas* to my publisher. I loved working on this book, but I loathed doing these acknowledgments because I am absolutely sure I have snubbed somebody or something really important. I humbly apologize for having a brain that can't find my cell phone or my coffee cup most mornings, just like the character of Hunter. If you read through it this far and you don't understand why I didn't mention you, it is because I'm an idiot. Please forgive me.

Thank you and I look forward to remembering you in my next acknowledgments, which will be for a book I am cleverly calling *The Untitled Sequel to A Dog's Way Home*.

W. Bruce Cameron
Los Angeles, CA
Tuesday, April 14, 2020